The Karakesh Chronicles
Book One

Tangled in Magic

Handersen Publishing, LLC
Lincoln, Nebraska

This book is a work of fiction. All characters, locales, and other incidents are a product of the author's imagination. Any resemblance to actual events, places, or persons, living or dead, is entirely coincidental.

Text copyright © 2017 Kim Ellis

Illustration copyright © 2017 Alison Gagne Hansen

Cover copyright © 2017 Handersen Publishing, LLC

Cover and Interior Design by Nichole Hansen

Summary: Agatha and Malcolm are twins separated by murder. Their only hope is to find each other, master magic, and reclaim their home. But the evil sorcerer Santer has a different plan.

Library of Congress Control Number: 2017900396

Handersen Publishing, LLC, Lincoln, Nebraska

ISBN-13: 9781941429518

Publisher Website: www.handersenpublishing.com
Publisher Email: editors@handersenpublishing.com

To Sebastian and Isabella,
for magical journeys

To Alex
with good wishes
Kim Ellis ♡

The Karakesh Chronicles

Book One

Tangled in Magic

Kim Ellis

Illustrations by Alison Gagne Hansen

Handersen Publishing LLC
Lincoln, Nebraska

Table of Contents

Part One

Chapter One
Agatha Flees Hawk Hill

Agatha strapped her dagger around her hips, preparing to escape from her childhood home. At fifteen, she refused to be married off against her will. Her uncle Chaucey may have considered Santer, his counselor, an acceptable husband, but she did not.

Santer was a half-warlock. He had left his apprenticeship early to manage Sir Chaucey's lands. Fifteen years younger than Chaucey, the counselor was still old in Agatha's eyes. He was a slim cobra of a man, given to wearing hooded tunics and sliding soundlessly through the stone hallways.

Agatha had always avoided his company. His slitted gaze made her uneasy. Everything about the older man repulsed her, from his yellowed teeth to the way he flicked his tongue like a snake.

She would not stay in the manse another day. Instead, she would run away to seek her twin brother, Malcolm.

Until today, Agatha believed her twin brother had drowned, along with their parents. But after a surprise visit from Aunt Viola, news of her brother set her head spinning.

Her twin brother could still be alive.

Agatha descended the spiral stairs in her soft boots. No one intercepted her. Chaucey and Santer were snoring at the oak table, their heads resting on their arms, legs flung out and loose. The strong sleeping potion she had dropped into their goblets after supper had done its work.

Sliding past them, Agatha paused for one last look at Chaucey, her guardian for the past three years. His beard, once reddish-brown, was now dull and threaded with gray. His eyes, even in rest, were wreathed in wrinkles.

"He was not unkind to me," Agatha thought, "but he did not care for me. He only cared for his dogs and his birds."

She didn't spare a glance for Santer, the counselor. Good at his job of managing the estate, the man was a snake in all other respects.

Agatha left through the scullery door.

By the light of the moon, she crept out to the stable of Hawk Hill Manse, and hastily tightened the girth on the

saddle of her gray mare, Manakshi—a gift from Aunt Viola for Agatha's fifteenth birthday.

Manakshi nuzzled Agatha's cloak looking for a treat while she fixed the saddlebags. She froze when the horse knocked into a wooden bucket. The clatter it made on the cobbles disturbed the birds in the mews.

She began to lead Manakshi past the mews to the stable door when there was a rush of beating wings.

Archer, her uncle's prize gyrfalcon, left her perch and landed on the grille. Agatha stifled a squeak of surprise. She stared nervously at the bird who stared back with unblinking onyx eyes.

"Take me with you," said Archer.

"I—I can't," Agatha said. Her mind jumped wildly from the surprise of a talking bird to the fear of her guardian's wrath. "You belong to Chaucey."

"Wrong," Archer said. "I belong to myself. Take me with you. You need my help."

Agatha shook her head. She pictured Chaucey chasing her down every path in all four directions. Though he might not trouble to follow Agatha, he wouldn't rest until he retrieved his much-valued bird.

"The key is in the tack room," Archer told her. "Open the grille now."

Minutes later, Agatha rubbed her eyes as if waking from a dream. She was amazed to find herself astride Manakshi in the moonlit woods with Archer perched on her right forearm.

Agatha's heart pounded three times faster than the horse's hoof beats. Not only had she made off with Chaucey's prize falcon, she had also taken his leather gloves along with Archer's hood, lines, and jesses.

As Archer had pointed out, Agatha couldn't be discovered traveling with a free bird. People would get suspicious.

They took the slim path that led to the northeast gate. The only sounds were the rhythmic thud of Manakshi's hooves and the faint jingle of Archer's ankle bells.

With her beak, Archer picked up a strand of Agatha's dark hair and tugged it gently before she spoke.

"I knew you would leave someday, Agatha," said Archer. "No fledgling could tolerate such solitude and such work. Why now?"

Agatha felt her throat tighten. She squeezed her eyes where tears swam. No one, not even Aunt Viola, had ever expressed concern over Agatha's life at the manse.

"How do you know about me?" Agatha asked.

Archer stretched out a wing. "My sight is sharp and long. Tell me, why are you leaving?"

"It's my brother, Malcolm," Agatha admitted. "A raven brought word to my Aunt Viola that he may still be alive. I have to know the truth. If he's alive, I have to find him. And Chaucey wants to marry me off to Santer."

"The man Chaucey's a pawn and a fool," said Archer. "And Santer is a scheming snake who will stop at nothing to gain Hawk Hill Manse for himself. I am glad to be shed of them both."

Agatha agreed with a shudder.

"And as for your brother," Archer continued, "we look where?"

"The wolf-headed woman in my dream said to ride to the north," Agatha explained. "My parents drowned where the two rivers meet. I thought I would start there."

Archer dipped her head, but didn't speak further.

Agatha decided to take the bird's silence as agreement. Two Rivers was many days' journey to the north. Would Chaucey and Santer pursue her?

Passing through the outer gate, Agatha urged Manakshi to a faster pace. In her mind, she reviewed the events that had driven her to leave Hawk Hill.

It had started with a curious dream two nights ago. A shadowy woman with the head of a wolf had said, "Ride to the north." Those had been her only words. Agatha had awakened, mystified by the dream. Now she understood that it had been a warning.

Archer
the Gyrfalcon

9

Chapter Two

Malcolm's Journal

My parents did not drown. They were murdered.

I was there and I saw what really happened. Mud was everywhere. We were wet to the bone from two days of riding in the rain. A hand-pulled barge took my parents and Santer across. There was no more room on the barge for my horse and me, so I waited on the shore with my old manservant, Oscar.

The river water was a dark, wicked brown. It roiled and snarled at our feet, carrying broken branches and an occasional dead animal. In the deepest and fastest part of the river, Santer took out his dirk and stabbed my mother's mount in its rump. The horse reared up in surprise. The shift in its weight upset the barge. Santer dropped to his knees. Holding onto the tow rope with one hand, he grabbed my mother's ankle. Then he toppled my poor mother into the waves.

My father fell off the barge when it tipped, but he managed to grab onto the side. He might have been able to save himself and crawl back onto the barge. Instead, Santer struck at my father's hands with the dirk as I watched helplessly from the shore. My father let go and went under.

The river swallowed both of my parents. Oscar leaned over to me and pulled hard on my cloak. He tugged several times before my horrified mind was able to attend to his words.

"Young master, you must flee. That evil monster Santer means to kill you, too. He ordered me to detain you, but I will not. Here, take this bag of provisions and go! Into the woods with you! Now!"

I was bewildered and too shocked to think. Oscar pushed the sack into my saddlebag, and slapped my horse's rear. It was all I could do to stay in the saddle as we galloped into the trees.

Asweil, my trusted horse, took me deep into the forest. I had to ride low on her neck to avoid the branches. Even so, when she finally stopped, my arms and legs bore scratches and deep scrapes. Three hard years have passed, but my arms still bear scars as a reminder of that terrible day.

I am writing this account of my adventures mainly as a diversion from the long evening hours here in the tower. And I admit, too, that I write with the faint hope that someone, some day, will read my tale. I no longer believe that anyone from home will find me.

After all, it is now three years since Santer killed my parents. I fear Chaucey and my sister must also have been put to death to make way for Santer to become lord of Hawk Hill, my parents' estate.

Zeddicus, the old man of the tower, provides me with all the paper I ask for. He gives me candles, too. It is no strain for him to use magic to bring these small utilities into existence.

After the evening meal, he plays his organetto. It is a rather cunning instrument, like a miniature church organ with pipes and bellows. He sits with it on his lap in front of the hearth where his fingers will stay warm.

While I wash the pans and wipe the table, the old man makes music. Sometimes he sings in his reedy, quavering voice. A stranger seeing him at his music would take him to be a gentle oldster, and maybe a bit soft in the head. Though he makes pretty music, in truth the old warlock's heart is as shriveled and dry as an autumn leaf. What a deception appearances can give!

For months I have been his slave, cooking and washing and carrying from morning to night. He is a sly and commanding taskmaster who holds me prisoner with his magic.

But I left off at the point when I was fleeing through the woods. The candle is guttering and I will not light another tonight.

Chapter Three

Scrub

There was only the wedge of moon as Manakshi moved through the forest. The horse seemed nervous, turning her head sharply to look from side to side. Her nostrils were wide with the scent of something that frightened her.

Agatha, in turn, felt anxious, and stared at the dark shapes of the trees where the horse kept looking. She saw nothing but an occasional flicker of a shadow, perhaps a branch lifted by the night breeze or—was it something else? Agatha feared they were being followed.

"Archer?" Agatha whispered to the gyrfalcon. "Do you see anything moving alongside us in the woods?"

Archer gave out a snort of derision. "Obviously you know nothing about raptors," she said. "We are diurnal hunters. We can see miles in daylight, and nothing in the dark. Have you ever seen a hawk or an eagle flying at night?

Of course not. Nighttime is owl time. We falcons own the sun."

They traveled on.

Agatha's head was drooping in half-slumber as the pastel light of dawn crept above the horizon. Now able to see, Archer launched herself into the air, and made a slow circle above Agatha. She returned a few minutes later, landing on a branch.

"I saw a rocky overhang near a stream," Archer said. "You can bed down there 'til dusk. There's grass for the horse as well."

Agatha longed for sleep.

"The sun is coming up. Shouldn't we keep going?" she asked the falcon.

"No, it's best to travel at night," Archer answered. "Let me scout our way in the daytime."

Agatha gave a sleepy nod and guided Manakshi off the path, following Archer's directions. Too tired to eat, Agatha rolled herself into her cloak in the recess below the rock. Leafy branches screened her from sight.

Still skittish, Manakshi cropped the grass, her ears swiveling forward and back. The horse's rhythmic munching quickly lulled Agatha to sleep. After only a couple of hours, Archer woke her by nipping at Agatha's arm.

"What is it?" Agatha mumbled, through a fog of sleep.

"Shhh! Listen!" Archer said, tilting her head.

Tap, tap, tap.

Agatha heard the sound. It was like the cobbler's hammer, nailing a boot.

Tap, tap, tap.

Sliding to her feet, Agatha followed the sound, moving from tree to tree.

At the edge of a clearing, she saw a girl.

It was hard to tell the child's age, as she was so thin, and wrapped in ragged clothes. The girl had a stone in her hand. She was banging it on the iron chain that linked her foot to a stake pounded into the ground. It was a feeble, futile effort, given the size of the girl and the size of the chain.

Agatha stepped out into the clearing.

The girl looked up in alarm.

Agatha put her finger to her lips, cautioning the girl to keep silent. Coming closer, Agatha saw that the iron band around the girl's ankle had cut through her skin. The leg was raw and bloody.

"Who put you here?" she asked, trying to keep the anger out of her voice. Not waiting for the answer, Agatha attempted to pull the stake from the ground. It was driven deep and didn't move.

16

"My da," the girl answered in a dry, thirsty whisper. Her eyes were huge in her pale, pointed face.

"Your father?" Agatha said. "Your father staked you out here?"

She examined the iron band and decided only a smith could release the metal.

"Too many girls, that's what my da says," the girl answered. "And I'm too weak to work in the mine."

"I'll be back," Agatha told her. "Don't make a sound. I'm going to get my horse. Manakshi should be able to shift that stake."

Manakshi stood patiently while Agatha improvised a hitch with her belt and some rope. The horse easily pulled the stake from the ground.

Agatha picked up the girl, stake, chain, and all, and set her astride Manakshi. They returned to the place beneath the rock where they could shelter in safety. She gave the girl some bread and cheese, and some swallows of cider.

"What's your name, little one?" Agatha asked.

"Scrub."

Agatha shook her head. "That's not a real name."

"That's what my mum calls me."

"It won't do," Agatha said. "Let me think of something more suitable while I wrap up your ankle."

With gentle hands, Agatha cushioned the girl's ankle with the extra leggings from her saddlebag.

"I have it. Let's call you Rami," Agatha said. "That's a strong name. I can tell you are a strong, brave girl."

The girl did not smile, but she nodded her head. "Rami," she whispered, trying it out.

Archer had been viewing the scene from her perch on Manakshi's saddle.

"Agatha, we cannot travel with a small, starving child," the gyrfalcon said. "Chaucey may already be looking for me, and Santer is a man of greed and purpose. He will come after you." The falcon spread her wings impatiently. "We are neither a charity nor a caravan."

Agatha looked from Archer to Rami, and back to Archer. Rami's eyes grew even wider.

"We must find a smith to remove these shackles," Agatha said, ignoring the bird's unfeeling words. "The child needs food and care. I want to take her to Sloane. Sloane will help. Can you see from above which way we should go?"

"I can already tell you that Sloane's farm lies to the south," Archer said. "That is, by the way, totally the opposite direction from north," Archer added with irritation. "In case you don't know your compass."

"I'm willing to take the risk to help Rami even if you're not," Agatha argued. "Please scout ahead for us. The farm can't be that far."

"I'll do it, but I warn you. You're losing precious time."

As the bird lifted up and away, she called, "I fear you'll regret this."

Agatha and Rami watched the falcon until she was only an arrow-shaped speck in the sky.

"Let's rest until she returns," Agatha said.

She lay down with her back against the stone, pulling Rami into the warm curve of her body.

"It's all right, little one," Agatha said as she settled Rami's head on her arm. "You're going to be fine."

When Archer returned, she brought supper in her sharp talons. Agatha roasted the fat pigeon beneath the rock ledge, concealing most of the smoke. While the two girls ate, Archer told them that Sloane's family farm was several miles to the south. To get there, they would have to leave the forest and cross open fields.

"It's a risk," Archer added, "even if we go by night."

Agatha's temper flared. "Would you really have me leave her here, shackled, and let her starve to death?"

Archer blinked her black eyes and remained silent.

"I won't do it," Agatha said. "We'll start at moonrise."

Chapter Four
Malcolm's Journal

Zeddicus is dozing by the fire. Even though he is not awake, his grip on the organetto is firm. It is the only thing here he seems to care about, except for his laboratory and his telescope.

But I shall resume my tale.

Asweil, my horse, took me deep into the forest. Eventually, she slowed to a walk. I was so tired by then that I made her stop. We found a sort of cavern beneath the spreading branches of a pine tree. I lay down on the dry needles. Asweil stood beside me and dozed. Her warm breath fluttered over my cheek from time to time.

When I awoke, I was hungry. In the bag Oscar gave me was a portion of dried beef, some journey bread, and a few apples. I ate only enough to ease my hunger. Then we went in search of water.

We walked for what felt like miles through the trees, and found nothing to drink. I ate another apple for the juice and I gave one to Asweil as well.

While we walked, I thought about my predicament. If I went back home, Santer would be waiting for me. I knew I was too young and too small to challenge him in combat, especially since he was skilled in magic. I would be unlikely to escape death at his hands. If I didn't go home, Santer would expect me to go on to our destination of Oxdenn Town, where my father's friend, the baron, was waiting for us. Though Santer might try to harm me, I might find protection there.

After hours of searching for either a proper path or water to drink, we'd become quite lost in the miles of trees. Asweil and I ate two more apples in the afternoon. I let the horse lead the way, hoping she would catch the scent of water. It was a wise choice on my part, for at sundown, she brought us to a thin, clear stream that trickled out of a tumble of rocks. We both drank our fill. Out of gratitude, I gave her the last apple. I ate the rest of the food, just a chunk of bread and some crumbled cheese. Then I rolled up in my cloak and slept.

Voices woke me.

Three odd little men surrounded Asweil. One stroked her nose while the other two examined her hooves. They were speaking to each other in excited squeaks.

"Such a fine horsie," said one with a crooked nose.

"Yes, yes, a fine, fine horsie," agreed another. He had big ears that stuck out under his hat.

All the men were about my size. All were clothed in yellow and green striped tunics with green leggings. Their skin was also a pale shade of green.

The third little man, who had a pointed green beard, grasped Asweil's reins. "This be a fine giftie for the Queen," he said.

"Yes, yes, a giftie for the Queen," the other two agreed. And they began to lead Asweil away,

"Hey!" I yelled, jumping up. "That's my horse!"

"Oooh! The little manikin is awake," said Crooked Nose.

"We're taking this fine horsie to the Queen," said Big Ears.

"We be the fine Grassmen, and we have a giftie for the Queen," said Beard.

"But it's my horse!" I said. "You can't take her. That's stealing!"

Crooked Nose laughed and clapped his hands. "Yes, yes, stealing!" he said. "We be the Grassmen and we be stealing your fine horsie."

Losing patience, I lunged forward to seize Asweil's reins

from Beard. He pushed me aside with surprising strength for someone his size.

"Oh, no, little manikin!" said Crooked Nose. He reached into a pouch on his belt and threw green powder at my face.

I was blinded. I coughed. Then the sneezing began, powerful sneezes that bent me double.

"Sneezie powder! Sneezie powder!" they all cried, laughing and clapping. "We gived the little manikin sneezie powder!"

My eyes were burning and streaming tears. I could barely catch my breath between the violent sneezes that came one after the other. Sightless, I waved my hands about, hoping to catch hold of something, be it horse or Grassman. But my fingers met only air. In moments, silence surrounded me.

Though I couldn't see, I could sense that I was alone. I stumbled my way to the stream and washed my face and eyes. Then I sat down with my back against a tree. Not only was Asweil gone, so were my mangle and my bow and quiver. All I had was my dirk strapped to my belt. The only thing I could think of to do now was to follow the stream because it might lead to a habitation.

And that is what I did. Hours later, the sneezes finally subsided, though my nose and throat continued to burn for another day.

Chapter Five

Sloane's Farm

With Archer standing guard, Agatha and Rami slept until the waxing moon nipped the horizon. Agatha wrapped Rami's metal restraints in her shawl so they did not jingle or clank. She put the child on the saddle in front of her. With Manakshi pressed to a faster pace, they left the forest after less than an hour's riding.

The North Star blinked on to guide them across fields of stubble and dried corn stalks. They covered the distance to Sloane's farm in one night. It was just getting light when the travelers hid themselves behind the barn. At last, Agatha saw a shadow moving back and forth across the farmhouse window.

"There she is!" Agatha whispered. "There's Sloane!"

Her heart beat fast at the thought of a reunion with her onetime protector. It was Sloane who took the blame when

Agatha burned the bread or left the wash out in the rain. Sloane made sure Agatha had enough to eat, and mended her stockings and tunics. Not often given to hugs or affectionate words, Sloane nevertheless made Agatha feel safer.

Santer had dismissed Sloane when he decided that Agatha was capable of doing the cooking by herself.

The first person to emerge from the door was a man. He was bear-like in his walk. His head seemed to sit directly on his shoulders with no neck in between. The man's arms bulged with muscle even though his hair was thin and silver. He entered the barn, and soon he could be heard talking to the animals inside.

Agatha and Rami waited in silence until, at last, Sloane stepped outdoors. She had a bucket in her hand. To Agatha, Sloane looked exactly as she remembered her, the stocky, round-breasted hen of a woman, fading blond hair pulled back under a ragged scarf. Her cheeks and nose were red-veined from too much cider, but the lines in her face were etched by smiles.

Agatha handed her horse's reins to Rami. She hurried forward, calling softly, "Sloane! It's Agatha!"

Sloane stopped, looked, then dropped the bucket and put her hand over her heart. "Agatha!" Sloane cried. "As I live and breathe!"

The next moment, Agatha was crushed against Sloane's expansive bosom. Agatha breathed in Sloane's familiar odors of sweat, smoke, and verbena.

Sloane grasped Agatha by the shoulders. She pushed her back so as to see Agatha's face.

"What brings you here?" Sloane asked with concern. "Oh, it does the heart good to see you! Come in, come in! How did you travel? Do you have a horse to stable?"

"I'll tell you all inside," Agatha said. "I hope you can help us."

"Us?" Sloane said. She looked behind Agatha, seeing nothing but the barnyard.

Agatha pulled Sloane behind the barn.

"This is Rami," Agatha said. "I found her in the forest."

Once Sloane heard Rami's story, her eyes flashed.

"There's no end to cruelty of folks, now, is there?" she said. "We'll have my man Lumper take care of these chains. Then I'll tend to your ankle, Rami. Agatha, go get Lumper from the barn. Tell him to bring his mallet and the iron wedge."

Agatha was amazed at the strength of old man Lumper. One blow of the mallet on the wedge severed the chain from the iron stake. Two more blows broke the bolt on the shackle, and Rami was free.

"She's as frail as a baby bird," Lumper said, lifting Rami in his massive arms and carrying her into the house.

Sloane clucked over Agatha's recital of her departure from the manse while making a salve for Rami's sores. She ladled bowls of rabbit stew for the girls.

When Agatha finally tore herself away from the comfort of Sloane's kitchen to check on Archer and Manakshi, she found that Lumper had brushed and fed the horse and bedded her in a dry stall with fresh straw.

"Thank you for taking care of her, Lumper," Agatha said. "Do you know where Archer is?"

Lumper grinned and pointed upward.

Archer was perched high on a rafter, feasting on a barn swallow. Cream and brown feathers floated down from above like autumn leaves.

Agatha returned to the warm kitchen where Rami dozed on Sloane's lap.

"All fed and comfortable," Agatha said, warming her hands by the stove. "It's so good to be here, Sloane. Even if Santer is after me, I'm glad we came."

Chapter Six

Malcolm's Journal

It was not easy to follow the stream. Sometimes it tumbled through steep, sharp rocks on rough hillsides. Sometimes, in flat places, it branched into many streamlets and I had to guess which course to follow.

Slowly, though, the water became deeper. The current grew stronger, and the channel wider. Staying by the water solved the problem of thirst, but I grew hungrier with each passing hour. I was, after all, only twelve years old, and used to substantial meals at home. Though a good shot with bow and mangle, I was not quick or skilled with throwing the knife. I remember taking aim at squirrels and rabbits, but I missed every time. I began to search for plants to eat.

There were plants on the banks of the stream. I knew some varieties might be edible, but I didn't know which ones. Several of the bushes bore berries, but there were none I recognized. I was reluctant to try any unfamiliar plants for fear of poisoning myself. Mushrooms grew in abundance. Those, I knew, could be fatal.

Much of the time that I was wandering along the stream, I thought about Agatha. Was she alive? Had Santer arranged her death? I never had trouble recalling my sister's face. All I had to do was gaze into a still pool at the stream's edge and there she was in my reflection. Same hair, the color of russet leaves. Same wide eyes, as brown as peat water.

When the hunger became too great, my mind grew confused. I imagined I heard Agatha calling my name. In my dreams, we challenged each other in target practice, or we shared a picnic of Sloane's roasted fowl and millet bread.

After three days of this wandering, I was weak and lightheaded. On the banks of the stream were plants that looked like the ones Sloane called wild carrots. I fell to digging up the roots. The taste was slightly bitter. Still, I ate five or so. Finally having some food in my stomach, I fell asleep beside the path. Less than an hour later, I was awakened by stomach cramps so severe that I couldn't get off my knees. Everything I had eaten came up. Then the retching continued until I lost consciousness.

Chapter Seven

Santer

After the meal, Sloane heated a kettle of water and gave Rami a bath. When Rami was freed of her rags, she looked more like a skeleton than a child.

"Don't you worry, Rami," Sloane said, "we'll fatten you up."

She covered Rami's wounds with dark brown paste. The salve smelled like a swamp, but it would speed the healing.

"The goddess must have heard my prayers," said Sloane. "Lumper and I have missed having a young one on the place. I needed a girl just like you to help me around the farm."

Rami's eyes never left Sloane's face. Her expression went from adoration to disbelief and back again. For the rest of the day, Rami limped after Sloane like a puppy dog, sometimes so close that she almost tangled herself in Sloane's skirts.

Agatha was sent up to the attic to prepare two straw pallets with sheets and blankets. While Rami rested by the hearth, Agatha helped Sloane with farm chores until sundown.

At suppertime, Sloane, Lumper, Agatha, and Rami seated themselves around the rough boards of the kitchen table. They all held hands at Sloane's insistence. She blessed the meal and smiled at the others.

"It's like I've got a family again," Sloane said, her eyes moist.

Agatha fell asleep holding Rami's hand. The brick chimney in their attic room brought warmth. Agatha slept more soundly than she had in years, warm and safe as a swaddled babe in mother's arms.

The next morning, Agatha was in the herb garden picking leaves for Sloane's winter supply. Archer sailed in from above, landing on a fence post.

"I've found a shortcut back to the northeastern road," Archer said. "Gather your foodstuff and supplies. We'll leave at dusk."

"Tonight?" Agatha paused, a sprig of thyme in her fingers. "But Sloane is going to show me how to prepare that ointment she made for Rami."

"Each day we delay is one day more in Santer's favor."

31

Agatha glared at Archer, but the bird simply stared back, waiting. Agatha turned her head away. She looked at the sprig of thyme in her hand through blurred eyes.

Must she leave so soon? There was so much comfort here, in Sloane's familiar presence. And in Rami's trusting fingers that grasped her hand before sleep. Not yet, Agatha's heart said, not yet.

"Just one more day," she said to Archer, still gazing at the thyme.

"Hmph!" Archer ruffled her feathers. "I'll fly up in a wider circle to see if someone is giving chase."

"Yes," Agatha answered in a low voice. All the while, her thoughts were of taking up permanent residence here at Sloane's farm. Sloane could teach her to make salves and potions, and Agatha could teach Rami her letters and numbers. There would be lambs and calves in the springtime. But she knew this was not possible, and that it would put Sloane and her family in danger.

While the sky was still light, the four of them—Agatha and Sloane, Lumper and Rami—sat down to an early supper. As Sloane set a pan of baked apples on the table, there came a sharp tapping on the window glass.

Archer peered in at them.

Agatha opened the door. The falcon flew inside and perched on the back of Agatha's chair.

All eyes were on the bird.

Archer drew out their waiting by preening her tail feathers.

Finally, the bird spoke. "Santer and his man, Reuven, are one day's ride from here. He's tracking you with his big hound, the one named Chisel. They'll be here by sundown tomorrow."

For several moments there was an angular silence. Then Sloane slapped her hand on the tabletop. Rami recoiled, startled by the sudden noise.

"Then you must leave, Agatha," Sloane said. "Tonight."

Agatha's heart slid down somewhere near her liver. "I—we—we could hide until they've gone." Her vision of a pleasant life on Sloane's farm wavered and dissolved, like morning mist.

"Not with a nose like Chisel's," Sloane said, shaking her head. "That dog could smell a rat under water. No, you must leave right away."

Agatha squeezed her hands into fists. She didn't move. Sloane got up and stood behind Agatha. She put her hands on Agatha's shoulders.

"Find your brother, Agatha," Sloane said. "Bring him back here, and you can stay as long as you like."

At the mention of Malcolm, his face swam into Agatha's mind. How she longed to be with him!

Lumper cleared his throat.

The large man rarely spoke, and when he did, it sounded like a rusty hinge on an old gate.

"She can't take the horse," Lumper said. "She'll get arrested for theft, with a fine horse and that gyrfalcon. I'll take the horse and disguise her. I'll put her out in the far pasture."

"Yes," said Sloane. "And Agatha can take Wee Boy to ride. He'll not draw attention. He's a sweet old donkey, very biddable. But what about the bird? How does she explain having the bird?" Sloane tapped her front teeth, thinking.

"Let her say she is taking the bird to a baron beyond Two Rivers Town," Lumper said. "A gift from her lord. She could be the daughter of the lord's falconer, perhaps."

"Yes, Lumper, that'll do quite well," said Sloane. "Agatha, go and pack your things. I'll make you a parcel of food to take along." She gave Agatha a gentle push. "Go on, now."

Up in the attic, Rami watched as Agatha rolled up her few garments and tucked them into one saddlebag.

"When you come back, will you teach me my letters?" Rami asked.

"Yes, little one," Agatha said, "and your numbers, too."

Agatha glanced around the cozy room that felt so safe for such a short time. If it weren't for the fact that her presence was bringing danger to Sloane's farm, Agatha might have argued to stay longer. The days ahead were sure to hold meals of cold food and beds on rocky ground, not to mention the threat of Santer. Agatha sighed, then heaved her bags over her shoulder and climbed down the ladder.

Chapter Eight

Malcolm's Journal

Before I continue my tale, I should describe the Towers where I live with the warlock. Three stone towers are joined together in a circle to form one tall building. The smallest tower houses the kitchen and storerooms. The middle tower is where banquets were once held. Above the banquet hall is the library.

My room is at the top of the middle tower. It is spare, but comfortable enough.

The tallest tower belongs to Zeddicus. He has his sleeping chamber there, and a laboratory. The topmost room is for sky-watching, with windows all around. I am allowed in the first two towers, but not in the third.

That door is always locked.

Outside there are two gardens. In one grow our vegetables and cooking herbs. The other garden is full of strange plants

that Zeddicus uses for potions and spells. It is tended by an aged badger who lives in a hollow tree at one end of the garden. Her name is Magda.

Magda, the badger, is one of the talking beasts. There aren't many of them left now. Magda is a surly, silent old thing. She certainly never talks to me. But, like me, Magda is trapped here by the warlock's magic.

Now, to return to my history.

I came to my senses with an aching, swirling head. I opened my eyes to darkness. The room I was in rocked and bumped. I smelled a strange, sweet odor, like burnt roses.

Next, I realized that I was warm and dry. When I wiggled my fingers I felt a blanket covering me.

As the fog left my brain, I determined that I was inside a wagon of some sort. When I tried to sit up, my belly gave me such pain that I quickly lay down again. I dozed until someone held a lantern above my face.

The lantern bearer was an ancient, dark-skinned woman. She had wrinkles upon wrinkles and a fine white moustache. Her head was wrapped in a faded flowered cloth. She peered at me with sharp, black, squirrel-like eyes. When she smiled, there was nothing in her mouth but pink gums.

"Who are you?" I said. "Where are you taking me?"

All I received in response was a confused look, then another toothless smile.

She said something to me in a language I did not know. We looked at each other for some moments. She took my wrist between her fingers and cocked her head, as if listening.

Next, a man came up beside her. They spoke together in soft voices. He was dark-skinned as well, not much taller than the old woman. He had a wild mass of graying hair and a long, droopy moustache. He leaned over me and studied my face. When he spoke, his breath was garlic.

"You boy, what's your name?" he asked me.

"Malcolm," I told him. It was an effort to speak. My throat felt raw and raspy. The old woman gave me a cup of sweet, warm tea that eased the soreness.

"You come from where?" the man asked.

"From Hawk Hill."

At the name of my home, I felt tears in my eyes. Father would have said I was too old to cry, but the struggle and sorrow of the last days overcame me.

"Your father and mother?"

My tears couldn't be held in. "Dead," I told him. "The counselor—Santer—he killed my parents." I turned my face to the wall and wept.

The two beside my berth spoke again in their language. The old woman brought a bowl beneath my nose. I breathed in that smoke of burnt roses.

Once more I slept.

When I woke again, sunlight fell through the curtained doorway of the wagon. My head was clear and I sat up to look around. The bed I slept in was built like a shelf into the side of the wagon.

Altogether, four berths with curtains were in the wagon, one more above me and two stacked on the other side. The colors of the curtains and bed covers were dazzling to the eyes, rich crimson next to golden yellow, bright turquoise, and deep violet. I had never seen such vivid colors. None of our dyers at home achieved such brilliance. Hanging from hooks and nails were all sorts of utilities. Lanterns, copper pots, and a variety of tools.

As I gazed about, a hand pushed aside the curtain on the berth opposite. Then a face looked out at me. It was the man I'd spoken to the night before.

"So the little man, he is awake! Malcolm, is it? From Hawk Hill?"

I nodded. My throat still felt rough and dry.

The man heaved himself off the bed and rolled on bowed legs to the doorway. He called out some words. Then he

returned with a skin bag of water. I drank and thanked him hoarsely.

The old woman came in with a steaming wooden bowl and a spoon.

By this time, I had swung my legs over the edge of the berth. She handed me the bowl and gestured for me to eat. It was some sort of spicy porridge, sweetened with berries. This food was the most delicious I'd ever had. When I'd finished eating, the woman grinned her toothless smile at me, took the bowl, and left. The man sat on the berth opposite me.

"Now, you Malcolm boy, you feel good, yes?" he said. "So you tell me who is this Santer who kill your mother and father?"

Today, were I in the same situation, I might be more cautious in what I revealed to strangers. But I was only twelve, half-starved, and mourning my parents. So I told the truth to the man, whose name was Yassif. I told about leaving Agatha at Hawk Hill, and the murder of my parents. I told how the Grassmen stole my horse, Asweil, and how I got sick from the roots.

All through my recounting, Yassif nodded his head, muttering, "Aah!" and "Hmm!" At the end, he said, "This counselor, this Santer, he is bad man. You go home, he kill you, too."

I sighed, too despairing to speak. What of Agatha? I wondered. And Sloane?

"I must think," said Yassif. "For now, you ride with us."

As it turned out, the "us" he referred to was part of the Tribe, a huge network of Travelers moving across the roads and forests of the country. In our group of Travelers, there were three wagons carrying a total of fourteen people.

Eventually, I learned all their names and sorted out who belonged in which wagon. Every person in the Tribe had jobs to do. At first, while I regained my strength, the old woman, Mata Jira, taught me to weave baskets and to carve eating bowls. These she sold in the villages and at the farms we passed.

Later, Yassif brought me with him to set snares and catch fish.

After some weeks, I began to look like one of the Tribe. My hair grew shaggy, and I was given clothing as my own wore out. Bathing was rare and we never washed our clothes. Had I not been burdened with sorrow and worry, I would have found it a great life.

On the Summer Solstice, the Tribe held the Gathering.

Most of the Travelers in the country met to celebrate the Solstice. It was at the Summer Gathering that Yassif first saw the panther.

Chapter Nine

Chisel

For Agatha, riding the donkey Wee Boy instead of Manakshi was like the difference between eating honey cake or hard tack. Her legs swung loose below the donkey's round belly, while the pad of blankets that served as a saddle did little to cushion his bony spine.

After some experimentation, Lumper and Agatha fashioned a perch for Archer on one of the saddlebags. This relieved Agatha from having to carry the falcon and endure hours of riding with the sharp talons clutching her arm.

When Agatha was ready to leave, Sloane hugged her tightly.

"You will find your brother, Agatha," said Sloane. "We'll be waiting for you both."

Agatha did not allow herself to look back at the three figures standing in front of the farmhouse as the donkey carried her away.

Sloane's farm lay at the edge of a long, narrow valley. Agatha guided Wee Boy along the road that skirted the western side. On her left rose a mountain covered in thick pine trees. On her right were fields of grain and pastures divided by stone walls.

As the moon, a half circle, rose above the land, Agatha kept watching the trees.

Wee Boy seemed to be nervous, continually looking toward the woods. Agatha was certain that a shadow flickered through the tree trunks, keeping pace. It couldn't be human. She was sure of that.

The shape was large, but not vertical. She listened while Wee Boy plodded along, but heard not a sound, no crackle of pine needles or twigs.

"If it's a predator, why doesn't it attack?" Agatha wondered.

After a long, weary night of travel, pale sunlight appeared above the trees. The path they were following widened into a regular carriage road. Agatha led Wee Boy into a thick grove of pine and laurel where they were well hidden, but not far from the road. Exhausted from the nighttime of travel and

the added nervous vigilance provoked by the shadow, Agatha rolled up in her cloak and slept.

Archer stretched her wings and took to the air to hunt and survey the land.

A few hours later, small ripping and cracking sounds awakened Agatha. Archer was back, and having her dinner. Between bites, she reported to Agatha.

"I flew back to Sloane's farm," Archer said. "She told me that Santer returned home to entertain some guests. He left Reuven and that monster of a hound, Chisel, to continue on your trail. They're moving fast. Faster than you. Reuven's riding that new mare."

Agatha was still sleep-fogged.

"What should we do?" she asked, rubbing her eyes.

"Move on now, in the daylight," Archer said. "We must keep on going through the night. Reuven likes his ale too much to pass up the pub in the next village. I wager he'll stop there, drink himself into a stupor, and rise late in the morning."

"Go by day?" Agatha asked.

"I've seen Chisel take apart a wild boar bigger than your donkey," Archer said. "You don't want to meet him."

"Do you think Chaucey would let Chisel attack me?" Agatha shivered.

"Chaucey wants me back. I don't think he cares how," Archer said. "As for Santer, if he can't marry you, your death puts him one move closer to his goal."

Agatha did not reply. She thought that perhaps Archer's opinion of herself was overblown. She got to her feet, replacing the saddlebags across Wee Boy's back.

Soon they were on the carriage road again.

Agatha urged Wee Boy to pick up his speed. The old donkey trotted for a few yards and then resumed his sedate pace.

The road before them began to steepen. Then it twisted in a series of curves that grew sharper as it ascended. Trees lined the road on either side of them and blocked the view.

Agatha could not see beyond the turn of the road in front and in back of her. The heat of the late afternoon, along with the rocking gait of the donkey, lulled Agatha into a half-doze.

Archer suddenly burst off her perch with a scream.

The gyrfalcon was brought to the ground by a net flung over her. Reuven, who had been waiting astride the mare around the next turn, gave a cry of triumph.

At the same time, Chisel came crashing out of the trees. He launched himself at Agatha. The last thing she saw before hitting the earth was the hound's red gaping mouth, ringed in white pointed teeth.

Agatha curled herself into a tight ball, protecting her head with her arms. She felt the heavy feet of the hound on top of her. She smelled his rank fur.

As quickly as Chisel took her down, his weight was gone. The air resounded with growls and the snap of jaws.

Agatha pushed up onto her elbows.

Two huge beasts grappled in the dust of the road. One was Chisel, with his studded leather collar. The other was a massive gray wolf.

Agatha scrambled backward, away from the fight. But it was over in moments. Chisel lay dead, his neck crooked and bleeding. The wolf turned and bared her teeth at Reuven, still seated on the mare.

Growling, the wolf stepped closer.

The horse reared, let out a whinnying scream, and galloped down the road with Reuven clinging to her neck.

The great wolf stared at Agatha with its ice blue eyes. Then the huge beast shimmered into gray smoke and vanished.

The Wolf

Chapter Ten

Malcolm's Journal

Yassif was out hunting deer illegally in the forest. He was not far from the huge field where all the wagons were parked. Waiting in a tree, with his bow drawn, he saw a three-point buck step into range.

When he was about to release his arrow, a huge black panther leapt out from the trees and took down the buck.

Trapped in the tree, Yassif watched as the panther ate its fill. Then it sat back on its haunches and licked its paws. That is when Yassif saw the snake tattoo on the big cat's footpad.

The panther had been conjured.

Mata Jira, who was herself a healer and a bit of a witch, built a special fire from bush wood. Then she read the flames. Yassif translated her words for me. The panther, she said, came from the north. And it was looking for me.

From that day forward, I was never left alone. If Yassif was not by my side, another man from the Tribe took his place until Yassif returned. I became alert to every movement and noise in the outdoors.

Sometimes a Tribe member reported seeing a large creature in the forest. But if it was the panther, it kept itself well hidden.

One day in early fall, the panther came back.

Yassif and I were checking snares in the woods. As was our habit, one stood guard while the other worked. This time Yassif was standing near me with his bow drawn. I was fiddling with the cords of the snare. I heard a snarl behind me and the twang of Yassif's bow.

Turning my head, I saw the panther collapsed on the ground. An arrow was lodged in its shoulder. It was mere paces from where I crouched, frozen with fear.

Yassif drew his bow again and shot the panther directly in the neck. The arrow pierced the jugular and blood spurted out. The big cat hissed. It struggled up and loped off lopsidedly into the darkness of the trees.

Yassif returned me to the safety of the wagon. Then he and several men of the Tribe tracked the cat to the river where the bloody trail ended. Had the animal tried to swim across? Was it dead?

No one could tell.

We only knew that there was no lifeless body to assure us.

For several days I was confined to the camp area. My restlessness finally annoyed Yassif so much that he let me go out with him again.

The months passed. We traveled through the Peaks and the Fens. Even such sorrow and despair as I carried decreased with the passage of time. My heartache changed shape, from a sharp arrow to a heavy stone.

Yassif and I talked many times about my predicament. We always came to the same conclusion, that I was safer on the move with the Tribe protecting me. Were I to travel on to my family's original destination, I could not be sure of a safe welcome. And going back to Hawk Hill Manse was sheer folly. I was not unhappy with the decision. Truth be told, I came to love Yassif and my life with the Tribe.

A full year went by, and once again we met the other travelers at the Summer Gathering. On the Summer Solstice, Yassif formally adopted me as his son. He gave me the necklace that I still wear. It is a medallion embossed with a fire symbol surrounded by stars.

Because I had reached the age of passage, I took part in a ceremony with several other boys. We were initiated into the Tribe as men.

Yassif gave me a bow and a quiver of arrows that he fashioned with his own hands. I had cause to use it soon enough.

The panther, we presumed, was still at large. It was searching for me. And the magical beast would not stop until I was dead.

Chapter Eleven
Wee Boy the Donkey

While the dust was still settling, Agatha felt her legs and ribs. She discovered that, although her body was bruised, no parts were bleeding or broken. Her legs shook so much that she was unable to stand. She crawled over to Archer, who appeared to be dead.

"Poor Archer," Agatha said.

Archer opened one bright eye. "Poor Archer indeed! Get me out of this thing!"

Agatha couldn't help grinning as she untangled Archer from the net. They were both alive, and Chisel was no longer a threat.

"That wolf saved us," Agatha said. "It killed Chisel and then it turned into smoke."

Archer, finally free, stretched out her wings and flapped experimentally. She began putting her feathers in order.

"Turned into smoke?" Archer said. "You're seeing things. And that fool donkey has run off."

Now Agatha realized that Wee Boy was gone. She looked along the roadside and detected a bit of trampled weed in one spot. Moving closer, she found a trail of smashed plants and broken twigs that led off into the trees.

"He went this way," Agatha said, and offered her arm to Archer. "Come on, let's go get him."

"Thank you, but I prefer to fly."

With Archer skimming above her from branch to branch, Agatha moved deeper into the forest. A clearing opened up before them. In it stood a curious dwelling, a circular tent made of skins. Wee Boy was there, chewing a mouthful of grass as if nothing had happened.

Agatha watched for some minutes from the edge of the clearing. Wee Boy had been hobbled with a frayed piece of rope. Agatha stepped cautiously forward.

Wee Boy looked up. He pricked his long ears in her direction.

Archer sat on a low branch in the shadow of the forest.

Agatha knelt down beside Wee Boy, beginning to work the knot loose with her fingers. She did not hear footsteps.

"Where are you going with my donkey?" a voice demanded.

Agatha turned and looked up.

The man was swarthy with a sagging black mustache and long stringy hair. He had on tall boots, knee breeches, and a stained linen tunic.

"This is my donkey, sir," Agatha said. "We were accosted on the road and he took fright and ran off."

"That's a sad tale," the man said with a scowl. "And a lie to boot." He took Agatha's arm and pulled her to her feet. "Now be off with you," he said, then shoved her toward the forest.

"This is my donkey," Agatha said more forcefully. "And you, sir, are the liar." She laid her hand on the dagger hanging on her hip. She wondered if she had the skill and courage to use it.

The curtain across the round tent's doorway moved aside. A woman shaped like a cider cask stepped out.

"Perchik!" she called. "The stew is ready."

The woman was draped in black cloth that fell around her in folds. Her head was wrapped in a red scarf. She wore large gold hoop earrings. Her face was as wrinkled as a winter apple, but her eyes were sharp and shiny black.

"What is this?" the woman asked. "A donkey and a girl?"

Agatha shook off the man's hand. She came forward and dropped a quick curtsy. "The donkey is mine, mistress. He ran off and I came to fetch him."

The old lady eyed Agatha, then the donkey, then the man. "And I suppose Perchik said the donkey was his."

"Yes, mistress, he did," Agatha said. "But it is not true."

Perchik glared at Agatha. "Mata, we could use a donkey. Let the girl find her way on foot."

"Perchik, my son, there are other reasons for encounters beyond acquisition," the woman said. "Come here, girl. Let me see your hand."

"My hand?" Agatha was confused by the turn of the conversation and the request.

The old woman nodded, causing her gold earrings to swing.

"Come here, girl," she said. "Perchik, go have your supper while it's hot."

Perchik scowled and muttered, but he went back into the tent.

Agatha gave her hand to the woman. The gnarled fingers glided over Agatha's upturned palm.

"Hmm, a long journey here," the old woman said as she traced a line. "And here—I see no parents. But here, a curious division. You—and another you. You have a twin?"

Agatha swallowed. "A brother. Yes, I have a brother."

"And it is him you seek on this journey?"

Agatha nodded. "Is he alive? Where can I find him?"

The old woman closed her eyes. "That I cannot see. Your future is clouded. Someone is trying to find you." The old woman's eyes turned sly. "We will keep the donkey. You will not need him."

"But I—" Agatha protested.

"Perchik!"

He was there in an instant, a long curved knife in one hand and a chunk of bread in the other.

"The girl is leaving," the old woman said. "The donkey stays with us. Give her the saddlebags."

Perchik tossed the saddlebags at Agatha's feet. She bent down to pick them up. When she looked back over her shoulder, Perchik, the old woman, the donkey, and even the tent—were gone.

Chapter Twelve

Malcolm's Journal

Zeddicus is going off to sell his potions in the town. I am left here with the animals. I have a plan to search the library for a book of spells. Dozens of books are stacked on the shelves. I will begin my search as soon as he leaves, and continue until he returns. Somewhere, in one of those volumes, I will find the counter-spell that will release me from this prison.

Zeddicus is a full warlock. Years ago he was Santer's teacher before Santer found employment as my father's counselor. Now Zeddicus holds me here, waiting for Santer's instructions. He tells me little, does Zeddicus.

But I do know that Santer hoped to marry Agatha and secure her share of the estate in a legal way. I overheard my parents discussing the match on our journey north. My mother was against it. My father was not so sure. Perhaps, after murdering my parents, Santer no longer required Agatha to wed. Has he killed her, too?

Three days have passed.

Sadly, I am no wiser regarding the release of the spell. But I have learned some useful magic. I know the words to unlock the door to the third tower.

There I spent an entertaining evening observing the heavens with Zeddicus's telescope. It made me feel very small, yet so terribly important at the same time. I also discovered how to make sparks to light a fire. That could be a most useful trick, but I must conceal it from Zeddicus. That means building up the kitchen fire in the usual, laborious way.

However, I did attempt a spell for Agatha because of the dream I had. Or was it a vision? So clearly did I see Agatha riding alone through a forest. I could tell she was in danger. I believed it was a vision, and that Agatha was still alive.

In the library, I looked for a way to conjure a protector for my sister. The spell I found was rather complicated, and I'm not at all sure that I said it correctly. I intended to send her a wolf spirit to ensure her safety. I may never know if I succeeded.

Zeddicus has returned. I will continue with my history.

During the winter, the Tribe limited their travels to the low country. One snowy day, Yassif and I went out to set

snares in the woods near our camp. I stood guard with my bow. Yassif sat on his heels, retying a snare.

We heard no footfalls in the soft snow, only the snarl. We turned at the same time.

The panther knocked me flat with a swipe of its clawed foot. Yassif leapt on the cat's back. He stabbed at the beast repeatedly.

The panther turned in a fury and attacked.

They rolled over and over in the snow, which became splattered with red. I drew my bow. For what seemed like an eternity, but was probably only seconds, I could not get a clear shot.

At last, the cat paused with its feet straddling Yassif. I shot my arrow straight at the heart.

The big cat fell.

Four Tribe men came running, armed with spears. They picked up Yassif and carried him back to the wagon. I followed, holding the shreds of my coat over my torn shoulder.

Mata Jira worked over Yassif for a long time. She could not assure me that he would live.

My own bodily wounds were superficial, and nothing compared to the pain in my heart. If Yassif died, it would be my fault, since my presence in the Tribe brought the panther.

As for that fearsome animal, it was gone when the men went back to retrieve its body. We were all sure that it had been dead when we left the scene of the attack. There was no trail of blood to follow as before. The beast had simply vanished.

To me, the decision was obvious. I was a danger to the Tribe, this kind and generous group of people who had adopted me. I had to leave.

While I waited to know if Yassif would live, I made my preparations. This time I would not travel unprotected. I packed food and the little clothing I had. I took all my weapons—the knife, the bow, and two quivers of arrows. I took a basket I wove so tightly that it held water. I sewed new, thick leather soles on my winter boots.

Finally, almost a full day later, Mata Jira came to me. She took my arm and pulled me into her wagon.

Yassif was alive, but his condition was shocking. His dark brown skin appeared gray. He looked small within the many blankets. The worst was his face, where only one eye remained. The other eye was bandaged with strips of linen.

Yassif was either drugged or unconscious. He did not know I was there. I smelled the same odor of burnt rose. It was Mata Jira's special herb that she used to bring healing and rest.

Mata Jira nodded in a knowing way and stepped out of the wagon. I took Yassif's hand, all scarred and scratched, and I wept.

"Goodbye, dear father," I whispered. "I love you too much to stay." Then I kissed his poor hand and his stubbly cheek.

That night, while the camp slept, I left.

Chapter Thirteen

The Panther

With her saddlebags slung over her shoulder, Agatha stumbled back to the main road. Archer flitted along behind her, keeping among the trees.

In the late afternoon, Agatha entered a small village. Having lost the donkey, she devised a plan with Archer to keep the falcon from a similar fate.

Archer waited high in a tree outside of the cluster of buildings while Agatha observed the activity from behind a shed. Outside the public house, several horses were tethered. She recognized the young mare that Reuven had been riding. The horse belonged to Chaucey. It was but a moment's work for Agatha to mount the horse and gallop out of the village.

Agatha hurried the horse northward during the night. At every bend in the road she expected another ambush.

Finally, as the light lifted in the sky, she retreated into the forest to rest. She found a sheltered spot under some bushes.

Before closing her eyes she said to Archer, "Now I'm twice guilty. I'm a horse thief *and* a bird thief."

"Ah, well," said Archer. "It's already done, so no use fretting." She fluffed her breast feathers. "I'm going to take a look up the road to make sure we're not being followed. Then I'll find something warm and tasty."

"Ugh," said Agatha. She wrapped the cloak tighter against the morning chill. She thought longingly of the cozy attic room at Sloane's farm.

"Someday I'll be there again," she promised herself, "and Malcolm will be there, too." He'd been alive when he sent the message with the raven. She just had to find him in time.

While she slept, she dreamt of her brother.

In her dream, Malcolm was tied with ropes on the floor of a cellar-like room. The shadow of a figure loomed over him as Malcolm struggled and called out to Agatha. Then she was running down a long, dim passageway, trying to reach him. But her feet moved as if dragging through slimy mud.

Agatha woke with a pounding heart and tears on her cheeks.

Archer returned at sundown. "There is a caravan heading our way. Horses, two supply wagons. It looks like a whole family is moving house. We must take care to stay hidden."

Agatha nodded in agreement. Her back was sore where she lay on rocks. Her mouth felt gummy, her eyes gritty, and her fingernails were dirty.

"I want a bath," Agatha said.

All she had to eat was the dry end of a loaf of bread and some molding cheese from Reuven's saddlebag. She sat up and gnawed at the hard crust.

"Archer," Agatha said, "I've been thinking. Chaucey and Santer may keep looking for us. The mare makes it easier for someone to follow our trail. Maybe we should trade her or sell her."

Archer was silent for several moments. "No, that won't do. Too many explanations will be needed. You want to stay hidden. I think a switching of horses is the best action to take. At the next habitation—farm or village—you can leave the mare and take another mount."

"You're right," Agatha said. She stood up and stretched. "It's sundown. Let's go."

The night of riding was uneventful. For the first few hours, Agatha remained tense and watchful. Later on, as the night waned, she hummed softly to stay awake.

Toward first light they passed by a well-endowed farm. Its rail fences were sturdy. Cows rested in one pasture. In another, three horses raised their heads. Chaucey's mare whinnied and pulled toward them. One of the farm horses trotted to the fence.

"Here's my chance," Agatha said to Archer.

First she took off the mare's saddle and bridle. Dismantling the rail fence was heavy work, but at last it was done. Agatha pushed the mare into the pasture. The new horse, a gelding, was not as young as the mare. He stood calmly as he was saddled and bridled.

"Maybe the farmer will think he's got the better bargain," Agatha whispered to Archer.

"That's certain," Archer said.

After another day of anxious sleep for Agatha, they traveled north until sunrise. Agatha's stomach growled. There was no food left. She grew lightheaded from hunger.

Agatha lay down in a grove of pine trees, but she was too hungry to rest well. She rose late in the afternoon.

The day was cloudy. A cold wind whistled through the pine branches.

Archer was out on her usual scouting and hunting mission.

While the falcon was away, Agatha washed in a slim stream. She drank water, hoping to fill her stomach and ease the hunger. Even though it was late in the fall, she looked for berries, but found none. She hoped Archer would come back with meat to share.

In the early evening, Agatha heard noises: voices, the jangle of bits, and the rumble of wagons.

It was surely the caravan Archer had seen. The sounds reminded Agatha of days gone by, when she rode with her parents.

Agatha prepared to travel again. She mounted the horse and waited for the falcon to appear. Staying concealed in the trees, Agatha watched the travelers approach.

Two men dressed like lords rode in front. They were followed by a wagon piled high with wooden chests.

Next came two women riding sidesaddle. One was richly clothed, the other wore plain rough brown linen. The second wagon passed by, this with sacks and baskets of foodstuffs.

Agatha considered raiding the supplies, but realized she couldn't be quick enough, given the size of the sacks.

At the end of the party rode an older manservant and a young boy in a cloak, mounted on a frisky horse. He was

having some difficulty controlling the animal. The manservant brought up his horse beside the boy's in order to catch hold of his reins. The boy seemed to refuse the help, so the manservant pulled ahead, leaving the boy to struggle with the horse.

Looking at the boy and the horse more closely, Agatha felt her heart thud. He was riding Chaucey's young mare, the animal that Agatha left in the farmer's field.

The youth appeared to be about twelve years old, the same age that her brother Malcolm was when he left on that long ago morning. He had light brown hair, not chestnut like Malcolm's. Still, he sat his horse with a straight back, just the way Malcolm did. The boy leaned forward over the mare's neck, speaking to her. The mare turned her ears back, as if listening. He patted her withers, shaded his eyes, and gazed across the road, directly at the grove of pine where Agatha was hiding. As she watched, Agatha noticed a shadow flicker among the trees on the opposite side of the road, just behind the boy.

What was it? She narrowed her eyes intently. Could it be the wolf?

Agatha gasped as the shadow formed itself into a lithe black body.

The panther leapt out of the trees. Then the beast crouched, ready to spring at the boy.

Agatha moved without thinking.

Kicking her horse to a gallop, Agatha pulled her mangle from its pouch. She set it whirling above her head and let go. The mangle wrapped itself around the big cat's neck, just as the panther launched itself toward the boy.

The caravan was in an uproar.

The manservant tried to steady the horses. The boy was frozen with shock. All the others were shouting.

The panther struggled to rise. It was stunned, but not dead.

One of the lords grabbed a sword and stabbed the beast.

The other well-dressed man rode to Agatha's side.

"Who are you?" the man asked, and then, "No matter, you saved my son. I am Harold of Green River. Our winter estate is just over the hill."

The man with the sword returned Agatha's mangle to her. She accepted it and slid it into the pouch. He was a younger man with a fair, friendly face.

"I am Harold's eldest son, Garret," he said. "You are quite skilled with the mangle, mistress."

The entire party surrounded Agatha.

Everyone talked at the same time.

The richly dressed woman was weeping.

"Goddess bless you, mistress," the woman repeated, while patting Agatha's arm.

Agatha herself was silent within the tornado of sound. She suspected that the panther's attack was meant for her or Malcolm. The boy had looked like a younger Malcolm as he'd sat astride Chaucey's mare. Agatha shuddered.

Finally, Harold quieted his household. "It is drawing dark. We have warm fires and supper waiting in the great house. Let's delay no longer."

Turning to Agatha, he said, "You will sup with us and stay the night. It is the least we can offer."

Agatha scanned the sky. No arrow-shaped bird was to be seen. Where could Archer be? Agatha didn't wish to refuse Harold's invitation and spend another night sitting in the cold dark with an empty stomach, waiting for the falcon. Food, a bed, and maybe even a bath outweighed any other choice.

"Yes, thank you, sir," Agatha said. "I will accept with pleasure."

Panther
Santer's Beast

Chapter Fourteen

Malcolm's Journal

At the edge of the camp, I paused to look back. Mata Jira found me there. I should not have been surprised, since she was a seer. She brushed my hair off my forehead and made some signs with her finger between my eyebrows, whispering incantations in her own language. She pressed something into my palm. Then she hugged me tightly, smiled her toothless grin, and stumped away toward her wagon.

There was enough light for me to see what I held in my hand. It was a small hexagonal box made of black wood with a hinged lid. When I opened it, I heard voices whispering.

A tiny, high, rustling voice said, "Owl alert! Owl alert!"

Then a bell-like call rang out, "Mouse in the grass, circle left!"

I closed the lid and then the voices ceased.

What a magical treasure this was! With the little box, I could understand the animals!

I tucked the box into my vest and strode into the woods.

My plan was to return to Hawk Hill. I knew I was far from home, way beyond Two Rivers. It would be a long journey.

For the first few days I managed well. One night I slept in a hollow tree. Another time I found shelter in a sheep shed where the sheep kept me warm.

When I needed food, it was easy to shoot a rabbit or squirrel. I became adept at climbing trees and hunting from the branches.

My fear was that Santer was still tracking me. I hoped to elude pursuit until I could reach Hawk Hill Manse and put an arrow through the man's evil heart. And only if he didn't conjure another panther, killing me first.

One evening, as I sat by my small fire under a willow tree, I cut some strips of bark and set them to soak in the stream. I began to weave a basket.

My fingers did not need much light to fashion the familiar shape, which I had practiced so often under the Tribe women's critical eyes.

As I worked, I hatched a plan.

I could make baskets and peddle them in exchange for bread or other supplies. With a trade to ply, I could keep to the roads and travel near habitations instead of avoiding them. The panther might be less likely to attack if I were among villagers and farming folk.

This proved to be my salvation throughout the winter months. Even during the worst weather, I found adequate shelter in barns and stables. I met many a kind person, and sold or traded enough baskets to keep me fed and shod.

Spring came with its rains and mud. One blustery, wet day I decided to cut through the woods where the earth was less sodden. Some miles into the trees, I came across a curious residence.

An iron grille painted yellow enclosed the house that was more of a hut with a roof of thatch. Smoke curled from the chimney, making the house look warm and inviting.

My own feet were cold and wet. As I considered the possibility of selling some baskets there, and perhaps warming myself by the fire, a thin old woman came around from behind the house. She saw me at once and came hurrying over to the gate. Her legs were more like sticks, with knobs for knees. When she smiled, she showed the biggest, whitest teeth I'd ever seen on a person that old.

"Well, well, a visitor!" she exclaimed. "You must be chilled. Come in, come in, young man."

She pulled open the gate. It creaked mournfully on its hinges.

"Good day, madam," I said. "I have fine willow baskets to sell."

"Come inside then, and let me see them," she said.

I followed her into the house.

A cat leapt up from where it lay on the hearthrug and ran under the cupboard. From there it peered out at me with slitted green eyes. The old woman told me to remove my wet boots and sit near the fire.

"May I offer you some warm cider and oatcake?" she asked. Her teeth were truly alarming when she smiled.

I agreed readily, being cold and hungry.

While she warmed the cider, I looked around the room. A table with two chairs, the cupboard, a cot with a blanket, and an overlarge oven were the only furnishings.

"My name is Jambedos," she said, handing me the mug of cider and a plate with four oatcakes.

I told her my name and thanked her for the food. The oatcakes were a bit dry, but the cider was sweet. Jambedos began telling me about her grandmother who had once lived in this very hut.

"My granny's parents were Travelers. They took her everywhere, crisscrossing the country year after year. She finally got tired of the wandering life and built this little house here in the woods. She liked to keep a few chickens, and sometimes a goat or two. We used to visit her every spring, right about this time of year."

On and on went the story. The room grew warmer. Soon I had trouble attending to Jambedos's tale. I tried hard to keep my eyes open, not wanting to be rude, but it was no use, and I fell asleep.

When I woke up, I felt cold and cramped. As I came to my senses, I realized that my feet were chained and locked together. Not only that, I was wearing nothing but my undergarments.

The cat sat directly in front of my face, staring at me intently. I thought that perhaps the cat might help me if I could understand its language.

My clothes lay in a pile out of reach, but I was able to wriggle close enough to catch hold of my vest. I took out my magic box and opened it.

The cat spoke, "She plans to eat you, you know."

You can imagine my alarm at this news. "Can you help me?" I asked the cat.

75

"Yes, I can help you escape, but only if you take me with you."

"I promise willingly," I said. "Where is the key?"

"She put it on the chair beside her cot," the cat told me. "It is too heavy for me to carry without making noise. You must fetch it yourself. Move carefully. You mustn't wake her."

It seemed to take hours for me to squirm and roll silently across the floor to the cot. I had to get on my knees in order to see the seat of the chair, and then I had to locate the key.

The cat was right in saying the key was large and heavy. But I saw something else on the seat of the chair—the old woman's big white teeth. Jambedos was asleep on her back with her mouth open, snoring loudly. Her gaping mouth revealed her real teeth. A shiver of horror ran up my back. Those teeth were like a wolf's, large and sharply pointed.

I used my vest to muffle the sound of the key as I unlocked the chains that held my ankles. Then I dressed and picked up my boots and pack.

With the cat riding on my shoulder, I slid out the door.

The gate was closed, and in my haste, I forgot how loudly it had creaked that afternoon. When I opened it, the noise woke the witch.

Jambedos dashed out the door and ran after me on her bony old legs. She ran very fast for an old lady. As she ran, she shrieked in fury and her wolf teeth glinted in the moonlight.

I soon realized that I would not be able to outrun the witch, especially with her unnatural speed. So I stopped next to a wide oak tree, then climbed up and sat on a high branch. The cat clawed her way to a limb above my head.

Jambedos stood at the bottom of the tree, glaring up at me with her hungry eyes and horrible teeth. She was beside herself with anger.

"Come down here," she screamed. "You're my dinner! Come down at once!"

With shaking hands, I loaded an arrow onto my bow. "If you do not leave now, I shall shoot you."

We stared at each other for a minute or more. I was ready to loose the arrow if she stepped any nearer.

At last, she shook her fists at me. She muttered something to herself, then stalked away into the woods.

I stayed in the tree for what seemed like hours, until I was sure the witch was gone and would not return.

Chapter Fifteen

Garret

All the way to the family's lodgings, Agatha pondered how much she should tell them. They seemed like good, kind folk. She continued to scan the sky for Archer, sometimes shading her eyes.

Garret brought his horse up beside her. "What are you looking for?" He looked up as well. "The weather is fair and will be tomorrow, too."

Agatha decided to tell the story concocted by Lumper and Sloane. "I've lost a falcon. She's my lord's bird. I am taking her to his friend beyond Two Rivers, as a gift."

"And your name, mistress?"

"Tarwyn," she answered, which was not a complete lie. It was her middle name, from her mother's mother. "My father is the falconer."

Garret said nothing, although his face had a quizzical look. He considered it unusual for a young woman to be traveling alone. Agatha sensed his disbelief, but she had no more story to offer him.

"The horse your little brother was riding," Agatha said. "She is quite lively."

Garret laughed. "Yes, she was giving him a bit of trouble at first. His own pony went lame shortly after we left for Green River. Father bought the new one from a farmer a day's ride past. He paid dearly for her, too."

As they neared Harold's lands, Archer was still absent.

The estate was about the same size as Hawk Hill, but it was much better kept. The hedges were trimmed and the steps to the great house were swept clean.

Inside, carpets and tapestries glowed with crimson and gold. Everything seemed to show a happy sense of caring. The woodwork was dusted and polished, and the pleasant scent of lavender filled the air.

The housekeeper, Felicina, greeted the travelers. She was a round butterball of a woman who spoke with an accent Agatha could not place. When she heard the events of the afternoon, Felicina threw her arms around Agatha in a tight hug.

"You save my dear boy!" she said. Then she kissed Agatha on both cheeks. Agatha blinked in surprise.

"Come with me, dear girl," said Felicina. To the young scullery maid watching from a doorway, she said, "Kenia, prepare a bath in the yellow room. And bring fresh towels."

The little maid scurried off.

Agatha was led upstairs to a room that was truly yellow. The walls were covered in tapestries whose color theme ranged from pale yellow to deep ochre. The carpets were daffodil and daisy patterns on a pale green background. It was the most luxurious chamber Agatha had ever seen.

Agatha had a hot bath, another rare event in her life. Bath water at home in Hawk Hill Manse was usually tepid by the time she had carried enough buckets to the tub in her attic room.

When Agatha came out of the bath much later, she found clean clothes spread out on the bed. The choice was between a high-waisted brocade gown or a linen tunic. The tunic and leggings almost fit. She gathered in the loose folds of the tunic with her belt, keeping her knife with her.

There was a knock on her door.

Agatha opened the door to Garret, who was also washed, and dressed in clean clothing. He paused to gaze at her with

admiration, causing her to blush. Then he led Agatha to supper.

The table was piled high with several types of cold meat, fresh bread, and a large bowl of apples and pears. Although she was ravenously hungry, Agatha only ate a small amount of the meal, knowing she must stay alert.

When her hunger was appeased, Agatha studied the faces around her. Lord Harold and his wife, Lady Rowena, sat at each end of the table. Next to Lady Rowena was a woman with sad eyes. Garret was on Agatha's left, and the boy, Cam, was on her right.

The rest of the people at the table were not part of the day's caravan. There were two more young men about Agatha's age whose names she didn't remember. They were engaged in teasing each other and bickering over a slice of venison. A young girl near Rami's age sat next to the sad-eyed lady.

Last, three girls slightly older than Agatha were picking at their food and stealing glances at her when they thought she wasn't looking.

Garret leaned close to Agatha. "The woman next to my mother is Lady Bethany. My uncle Arnolf died last spring in a hunting accident, so his family resides with us. The two boys, William and Walter, are her sons. They argue like that

all the time. The little girl is Delia, the youngest of my cousins. Of the three girls staring at you, the one with the dark hair is my sister, Gwyndar. The other two are our cousins Tamara and Solvi."

"So many!" Agatha said. "How shall I remember them all?"

The meal was taken at a leisurely pace, with much talk and retelling of the panther's attack. When all the plates held only bones and apple cores and breadcrumbs, Oswald, the manservant, hurried into the hall. He whispered urgently to Lord Harold.

"Bring the beast in here," Agatha heard Lord Harold say. "I'm sure we'd all like to behold this curiosity."

Oswald returned with another man, both dragging a canvas on which lay the body of the panther. The family crowded close as Oswald raised the front right paw of the big cat. Tattooed on the footpad was a hooded cobra poised to strike.

At the sight of the snake figure, Agatha's knees weakened and she swayed.

The symbol belonged to Santer. He wore the same design on his tunic and on a gold pendant. As Agatha suspected, the counselor was seeking her death. Agatha reached behind to

steady herself. Garret was quickly beside her, and supported her with an arm around her shoulders.

"What is it, Tarwyn? Do you feel faint?" Garret helped Agatha to a seat.

"The panther—" she said. "It's so big."

Garret gave her another puzzled look as he handed her a cup of water.

Agatha could sense his disbelief, but she remained silent. She imagined that he must be wondering how a girl who earlier displayed courage and skill with a weapon now grew faint at the sight of the beast she'd taken down.

"Mistress Tarwyn is fatigued," Garret said to the family. "I'm taking her to her chamber."

At the door to the yellow room, Agatha paused. "I must look for my falcon tomorrow. She will be searching for me."

Garret nodded. "I will ride out with you. And will you show me how to throw that weapon of yours?"

Agatha smiled. "Yes, I'd like that." To her surprise, he kissed her hand.

"Goodnight, mistress," he said. Agatha retreated to her room with warm cheeks.

Chapter Sixteen

Malcolm's Journal

Rowl, the cat, proved to be a pleasant and useful companion. Being a nocturnal animal by nature, she kept watch at night while I slept.

As we journeyed south, I told her my story. If she wanted to speak, she patted the place on my vest where I kept the magic box. But Rowl was not a chatty type, which suited me well. She only spoke when she felt it was necessary.

Spring gave way to the heat of summer days. Continuing to make my way toward home, I sometimes hired myself out as a day worker at farms. In return for my labor, the farmers gave me meals and a place to sleep.

I walked from one village to another. Some villages were well appointed, with a green commons and a shop or two. Others, the mining villages in particular, were dull and downtrodden, with only a scattering of shabby huts.

All the while, I thought about Agatha. I wondered if she were still alive, and if so, would Chaucey have married her off?

One afternoon, as we made our way along a well-travelled road, I chanced to see three towers rising above the forest to the west. Thinking I might find shelter for the night, and perhaps sell some baskets, I turned off the road onto a path that led in that direction.

It was already sunset when I came to the clearing with the three towers. I saw the two gardens of which I have already written.

From inside the towers, dogs began to bark. Rowl hopped off my shoulder and quickly scaled a tree. From her perch, she nodded at me to go ahead and that she would wait for me in safety. Little did I know that it was the last time I would see her. I never did find out what happened to Rowl. I looked for her every day as long as I remained at the Towers.

An old man opened the door to my knock. He looked me up and down for some time before stepping aside to motion me into the first tower. His conversation was civil enough, though he spoke without elaboration. He told me that his name was Zeddicus, and that he was an herbalist.

My appearance, he said, was fortunate, for he needed some assistance with some heavy work that he could not manage himself.

"Would you be able to spare me a day or two?" he asked. "I'll give you your meals and a warm place to sleep."

I did not answer right away, as I recalled my unpleasant encounter with the witch Jambedos. I studied the old man. He appeared rather frail. The bunches of dried herbs arrayed on the walls supported his claim of profession. The scent and bubble of soup cooking in a kettle decided me.

"One day," I agreed, "but then I must travel on."

We shared a simple but substantial supper of meat soup and brown bread.

"Do you mind doing the washing up?" he asked me with a thin smile. "I usually play my organetto in the evenings."

Since he was my host, I had no objection to washing our plates and cups and wiping off the table.

While I worked, Zeddicus brought out his instrument. He held it with such care that it was like a mother's caress. The music he made was unlike any I had heard before. I sat by the hearth fire and listened until he wearied and went to his bed.

The next day, I did several tasks for him. First I weeded and hoed the herb garden. I was surprised to see the badger gardening in the adjacent plot.

After my experience with Jambedos the witch, I should have been wary, but I was not ill at ease. To me, Zeddicus appeared only as a slightly eccentric, lonely old man. In the afternoon, he had me split and stack wood for the fire. That night, we shared another satisfying meal of stew and roasted potatoes. Again, Zeddicus played his organetto.

On the second day, Zeddicus showed me how to bake the brown bread. I made seven loaves, one for each day of the coming week. I killed, cleaned, and cooked a chicken. By midafternoon, I was tired of doing the old man's housework, and so I picked up my pack. I found Zeddicus in the library, muttering to himself over a dusty volume.

"Sir, I thank you for your hospitality, but I must continue on to my destination."

He looked at me with his pale blue eyes and said, "You can't go."

"I'm sorry, sir, but I must leave," I said. "I have tasks waiting for me elsewhere."

"No," he said, shaking his head. "You really can't leave."

"Well, I must. I'm going now," I answered, and I strode out the door and down the front path toward the forest.

When I got to the edge of the clearing around the Towers, I felt a twisting around my neck, as if a kerchief were being pulled too tight. I kept walking forward, and with each step,

the constriction around my neck increased until I was gasping for breath. Not understanding, I kept staggering away from the Towers until finally I passed out from suffocation.

When I came to, I was lying on the ground in front of the Tower steps. I don't know how I got back there. Perhaps Zeddicus dragged me.

Again, I attempted to leave the clearing, and again I could not breathe. This time, though, I stepped backward and I felt the invisible noose loosen.

Forward, tighter, backward, looser.

I tried all the points of the compass. No matter which direction I essayed, I began to choke. In the end, I sat down on the Tower steps and rubbed my aching throat.

The door opened behind me.

Zeddicus looked down at me with an amused smile on his lips. "You see," he said. "You can't leave."

"What have you done to me?" My head ached from having my air cut off so many times. "Why are you keeping me prisoner? I have done you no harm."

"A former student of mine asked me to detain you," he told me. "I am delighted that I can still do the chaining spell. I was afraid I'd grown rusty after all these years at the Towers."

"Is there a counter-spell also?" I asked, drawing my knife. "Because I think you need to remember it right now."

"There is always a counter-spell," Zeddicus answered. "But I don't think we need it."

He made a curling motion in the air with his fingers, and the invisible noose squeezed my neck tight enough to make me see stars. I dropped the knife.

When I could breathe again, I said, "Who is this student of yours? What am I to him?"

"Ah, the gentleman goes by the name of Santer," Zeddicus told me. "He asked me to delay you until after the wedding."

"What wedding?" I said, but I already knew.

"Santer is to marry your sister as soon as she comes of age this summer," Zeddicus confirmed. "And then he will dispatch you himself. Apparently other efforts to do so have failed."

Knowing that Agatha was still alive lifted my spirits.

With the chaining spell, the old man was able to force me to do his bidding. If I was too slow, he wiggled his fingers and the noose tightened. If I was tired and resisted a demand, my breath was stopped.

One morning, as I worked, I wondered if Agatha was also a prisoner. I could not imagine that Agatha would cooperate in this marriage unless she, too, were a victim of the chaining spell. But I knew my sister. She would scheme and resist. She would find a way to escape.

The thought of Agatha gave me strength to scheme as well. Already I knew that the chaining spell surrounded the property, and there was no crossing it. I had to find the counter-spell. I had to pretend compliance, and find a way to escape.

Chapter Seventeen

Green River

When she awoke the next morning, Agatha lay under the quilt, taking in the brilliant colors of the tapestries. The chamber was so richly furnished that it could have belonged to a princess. Her own room at Hawk Hill Manse was pleasant when her parents were alive, but nothing like Lord Harold's home.

Agatha stretched and yawned.

Too soon, the previous day's events intruded on her comfort: the panther, the cobra tattoo, Garret. And Archer.

"Archer!" Agatha sat up, clutching the sheet to her chest. She must get up and ride out to search for the bird.

Now fully awake, Agatha remembered the shred of a dream. Archer was perched atop a stone pillar, glaring at her with those accusing yellow-ringed eyes.

Agatha washed quickly, then looked for the clothing she wore last night. The tunic and leggings were not where she put them. Instead she saw a day gown of embroidered linen.

"I can't ride in this," Agatha said.

She opened the wardrobe where her old, worn garments were neatly folded. She put them on.

Strapping on her belt with the knife, and slinging her mangle over her shoulder, she made her way through the corridors to the dining hall, and breakfast. Only Garret and Lord Harold were at the table. Their expressions were serious. They were speaking in low voices, but they ceased talking when Agatha entered.

"You slept well?" Lord Harold asked. "The chamber suits you?"

Agatha assured him that she was comfortable. Judging by their worried faces, she knew something was wrong.

"Is something amiss?" Agatha asked. "Is someone ill?"

The men exchanged questioning looks. Garret nodded to Lord Harold that he should speak.

"The panther has disappeared," Lord Harold said.

Agatha stiffened. "But it was dead."

"So we thought," Lord Harold agreed. "The body was left in the root cellar until the men could bury it this morning. When they went to retrieve it, the panther was

92

gone." Lord Harold shook his head. "We are mystified. Have you any explanation, mistress?"

Agatha shook her head.

"There is a feeling of dark magic here," Lord Harold said. "I've sent a messenger for the magus. Perhaps he can tell us what this means."

Agatha was thrown into confusion. If the magus were skilled, he might divine the truth of her journey. She must find the falcon and leave.

"I have to go search for Archer," Agatha said. Hurriedly, she put an apple and a chunk of bread in her pouch.

"Wait a moment," Garret said. He gulped down the last of his cider. "I'll come with you."

At the stable, Garret and Agatha saddled the horses. The morning was still damp with dew as they trotted out of the gates. Agatha shaded her eyes from the sudden bright light. The sky was a clear, cloudless, bird-less blue.

After they had circled the fields of the estate with no sign of the bird, they rode back along the road where Agatha met the caravan.

"Falcons have amazing eyesight," Garret said. "If your bird were anywhere nearby, she would see you."

Along the way, they stopped to let the horses drink at the pasture stream. Agatha ate her apple and let her mind drift.

She was enjoying this respite of comfort and safety. But her thoughts kept returning to the cobra tattoo. Santer, she realized, might have more magic skills than he had revealed. Could the panther have been revived by magic?

Suddenly she became aware of Garret talking to her.

"Tarwyn, I've said your name three times."

Agatha's face flushed. She turned away, unable to think of an explanation.

"That's not your name, is it?" Garret asked. "Who are you, really?" He reached for her hand. "You can trust me. Why did you swoon over the cobra sign?"

Agatha's heart was pounding. Like a cornered beast, she didn't know how to escape Garret's question—or what to do with the feel of his hand holding hers.

The need for a decision was swept away in the beat of Archer's wings as the falcon swooped within inches of Garret's head.

Agatha leapt to her feet, crying, "Archer! Here, Archer!"

The bird soared up and turned a tight circle. She made another pass at Garret, talons spread to strike. He ducked in time to feel the wing feathers sweep his hair.

In wordless agreement, Agatha and Garret mounted their horses and gave chase.

At the edge of the pasture, Archer was gone. They waited for some minutes, scanning the sky and the trees.

Agatha shook her head. "She won't come back today. She's angry. Tomorrow I'll come alone."

Agatha and Garret turned toward the gatehouse. They saw several horses with riders coming toward them through the gate. William and Walter were in front, tearing along at a mad gallop.

"I won!" yelled William, flying past in a cloud of dust.

"No, I won!" Walter shouted. He aimed a slap at William's head, but his brother moved out of reach.

The boys slowed their horses to a walk, turning toward Garret and Agatha.

"Garret! Tarwyn!" William called. "Felicina made a gorgeous picnic for us. The girls are coming with three hampers."

"And Cam has two blankets," said Walter. "Let's spread out on the sky rock."

"No, there are too many ants," William said. "Let's sit by the stream."

"Sky rock."

"Stream."

"Sky rock."

"Enough, you two," Garret interrupted. "I'm the oldest, and I choose the wide oak. We'll have shade and no ants."

William and Walter made faces at each other.

Walter yelled, "Race you to the oak!"

Off they went in a clatter of hooves. Agatha caught Garret's eye and laughed.

"Are they always competing?" Agatha asked.

"Always," Garret said. "Look, here come the girls."

Agatha remembered that Garret's sister was the dark-haired one named Gwyndar. She was wearing a white cap over her hair. She was slim like her brother, but her teeth protruded in a rabbity way. Tamara and Solvi looked like their mother. They had large brown eyes that drooped slightly at the edges. Their faces were round and friendly.

"What a fine day for a picnic!" Solvi said.

Cam was the last to join them. He was again riding Reuven's young mare. Agatha noted that Cam seemed to have convinced the horse that he was the master. She felt a pang of loss as she was reminded of Malcolm.

That night, Agatha lay in her soft bed, smiling. She couldn't remember the last time she'd felt this happy. Maybe a long time ago, when Malcolm and she were little, when their parents were alive, and she felt loved and safe.

The afternoon picnic had been full of talk and laughter. Delia played with Agatha's hair. William and Walter argued over the last meat pie, the last chicken leg, and also the last honey cake. The others just ignored the scrapping boys. Cam had put a spider down Tamara's bodice, which he regretted when she smashed his piece of honey cake into the dirt. And whenever Agatha looked up, she found Garret's eyes studying her.

After the lunch leavings were packed away, Agatha had been persuaded to teach them how to throw the mangle. Everyone, even the girls, wanted to try.

There was a lot of running back and forth to fetch the mangle. Gwyndar surprised all of them by quickly learning the knack of throwing the weapon.

Finally, hot and sweaty, they had walked into the shady woods to pick hickory nuts. The girls carried full aprons back to the oak tree where they all sat about cracking nuts and picking out the meat with twigs.

While Agatha was bent over her lap and poking at a hickory nut, Garret leaned close. "Your hair is so beautiful. It's the color of polished Cherrywood."

Agatha's face grew hot. She glanced up at him, and then bent over her task again. Should she hide her appreciation of

97

his fair features and his kindness? Such flirting was new to her.

Of course the cousins had been curious about Agatha's home and family. Agatha let her imagination flow freely to answer their questions. Her father, she said, was the falconer for Baron De Wilde.

In truth, the Baron's estate did border the manse at Hawk Hill. Baron de Wilde also had a falconer named Charlie. He was an aged man whose children had children.

In Agatha's telling, Charlie was her father. Her mother was dead, but she had a younger brother, Matten. Agatha added that a manservant and his wife had accompanied her on the journey to deliver the falcon, but the man had fallen ill. She left them both in a town some days back and continued on toward Two Rivers in order to arrive ahead of colder weather.

It was a grand tale she wove. She had quite enjoyed creating it. Her audience was rapt and wide-eyed. All but Garret, who had listened to her with his head cocked and eyes narrowed.

When the afternoon sun dropped low and the air grew chill, the picnickers had returned to the manse. As Agatha was washing up in her room, all three girls, along with little Delia, piled in chattering like finches. Solvi fashioned

Agatha's hair with braids and combs. Gwyndar laid out a crimson and indigo gown of her own for Agatha to wear that evening.

Delia sat on Agatha's lap while Solvi fixed Agatha's hair. The warm weight of the child felt like comfort itself. Solvi's hands plaiting her hair were soothing. The girls chatted about the picnic, and how Garret couldn't keep his eyes off "Tarwyn."

At dinner, Agatha had to tell her tale again. She worried that she would make a mistake in the telling, and be caught. She was aware of Garret's gaze. This time she was bold enough to meet his eyes a few times, and offer a smile. When he smiled back, Agatha's heart hopped.

When the meal was over, they had all moved into the library, where Lord Harold and the two ladies played cards. The children made themselves comfortable on the hearthrugs in front of the fire. They played tiddlywinks and lotto. Delia fell asleep with her head on Agatha's lap.

Finally, the fire burned low and they all trooped off to bed. Garret had walked Agatha to her door.

"That was quite a tale you told today," he said, taking her hand.

"A tale?" Agatha pretended confusion.

"You're so mysterious, full of contradictions," Garret said. "You're brave and strong, and then you make up false histories. I am quite intrigued." He kissed her hand and then her cheek. "Goodnight, lovely."

Agatha hurried into the yellow room.

Dare she admit that she had a suitor? It was all so new to her, this life of play and pleasure. But it could end abruptly if the magus revealed her true identity and purpose.

In spite of that worry, Agatha fell asleep smiling.

Chapter Eighteen
Malcolm's Journal

One of the first efforts I made to escape was to use my magic box. I thought that if I could communicate with the animals at the Towers, I might learn something that would be of help.

Zeddicus had two big dogs that spent most of their time roaming the woods. The chaining spell had no effect on them, so they could pass across the barrier unimpeded.

One day when Zeddicus was in his laboratory, and the dogs were lying in the shade of a pear tree, I brought out my box and opened it. This is what transpired between the two dogs.

"Hot today."

"Hot."

"I smell squirrel."

"No, rabbit."

I knelt beside them and said, "Can you help me escape?"

"Why? He feeds you."

"I smell rabbit."

"No, squirrel."

"Is there a way past the chaining spell barrier?" I asked, growing frustrated.

"What barrier?"

"I smell rabbit."

I gave up on the dogs. I closed the magic box. Obviously no help was coming from those pea-brained animals.

Another of my efforts was to seek entry into locked rooms. Wherever I went in the Towers, I tested doors. Someday, I reasoned, Zeddicus would make a mistake and leave one open. After all, he was old and forgetful. He often asked me to find his spectacles or a book he had put down somewhere.

Then came my chance.

Several days after my imprisonment, Zeddicus left a door unlocked. It was the one leading underneath the second tower. I hurried on quiet feet down the steps, a candle in my hand.

The rooms below were more like cells, dark caverns with rusty grilles across their openings. I wondered if perhaps this had been a dungeon in earlier days. I thought all the cells were unoccupied. Then I heard a snarl that almost stopped my heart with fear.

102

In the flickering light I saw the panther.

It pushed its huge black head against the bars. My candle's flame lit the white fangs and reflected red in the cat's eyes. One massive paw, with its enormous, sharp claws, extended through the bars. Of course, on its footpad was the cobra tattoo.

At first, I was too terrified to move.

I almost dropped the candle.

The panther lunged against the iron grille, trying to reach me through the bars.

Staying at a safe distance, I took a closer look. There was a white scar on the beast's neck. Another showed directly over its heart. Then I knew that it was the same animal I had shot, the one that had almost killed Yassif.

I could barely breathe.

When I was able to use my legs again, I went backward up the stairs and shut the door. Then I sank to the floor, trembling violently. It was as if my death were living beneath me, waiting to be released. Was there a way to destroy a beast that had been conjured by magic?

That evening I heard the dogs fighting. They often did this, when one caught a squirrel or rabbit and the other wanted a share. The only solution was to take the prey and divide it. If not, they would continue the disturbance indefinitely.

I found them in their favorite spot beneath the pear tree. The victim this time was a young raven. Its coal black feathers were wet and slimy from the dogs' mouths.

"Down!" I shouted. The two dogs glared at me, but hunkered down on their bellies. "Drop it!" I commanded.

The one with the bird in its mouth would not obey.

At that moment, the raven opened one eye and said, "Help me."

The dog did not want to release its prey. I was not on such good terms with these dim-witted canines that I felt comfortable with my fingers near their mouths. In the end, though, I had to pry the animal's teeth apart. I took the soggy bird to my chamber. On closer inspection, I saw that one wing was broken.

As I fixed a splint to the bone, I asked the bird, "How did you come to get caught by those two foolish dogs?"

"It is not an event that I wish to discuss," the bird answered. "Suffice to say that I made an error in judgment."

The raven gave his name as Carl the Third. "I am the proud descendant of Carl the Second, descendant of Carl the First, one of an illustrious line of the ravens that guard the castle gate of the king's court at Karakesh."

"You must stay here in my room until your wing has healed," I told the bird. "And then you should flee, for if

Zeddicus discovers you, the old man may take you prisoner, as he has done with Magda the badger. And me."

"You're a prisoner?" the bird asked. "Tell me how this came to pass."

So I told Carl the Third my story.

Afterward, he helped me make a plan. But we had to wait until Carl the Third was able to fly again.

In the meantime, when I was not being forced to work long hours, I spent my free minutes in the library, searching for maps of the country. I found several that, when put next to each other, gave me an idea of where the Towers were located. Zeddicus had told me the name of the town where he sold his potions and herbs—Calinia.

I suppose he thought that he had me trapped, and that knowledge of the area would make no difference in my situation, as long as he was in control.

I was able to find Calinia on a map. The Towers were northwest of Two Rivers, and I knew that Two Rivers was several days of long riding from Hawk Hill. To the southeast of Hawk Hill Manse was Keystone, where my Aunt Viola lived. That is where I sent Carl the Third when his wing healed.

The panther's presence put me in a state of nerves. During the nights, I lay awake, wondering how I could escape. One night, after I had finally fallen asleep, I had a dream. The

dream showed me a figure surrounded by a ring of fire. It was a woman with the head of a wolf. She stepped through the fire.

"Talk to the badger," the wolf-woman said to me.

Then she stepped backward, and disappeared in the flames.

I woke to the sound of Carl the Third tapping on my window. I let him in and he pranced about on the ledge. He was so proud of himself to have accomplished his errand that I couldn't get any sense out of him at first.

Finally, I understood that he had found my Aunt Viola. He had given her the news that I was alive. Aunt Viola had been about to leave for Hawk Hill Manse to celebrate Agatha's fifteenth birthday. It was mine as well, but the day had slipped my notice. Our aunt said she'd speak privately to Agatha. On the way back to the Towers, Carl met a falcon.

"Big bird, rather arrogant and condescending. Said her name was something...hmmm...Searcher? Arthur?" Carl the Third scratched his head, trying to recall. "Oh, well. We had a bit of a chat. I told her about my mission and your imprisonment. She said she was traveling with your sister, looking for you."

"Could it be Archer? Chaucey's gyrfalcon?"

"Archer! Yes, that's the very bird. I had to bring you a message. Let me see, she said to tell you that if you should

escape before they get to the Towers, you should wait at...hmmm...I had the name a moment ago...at a river. One river?"

"Two Rivers?" I asked.

"That's it! Two Rivers."

"But how shall I escape from this place?" Then I told Carl the Third about the panther in the dungeon, and my dream.

"Come, come," said the raven, hopping onto the bedpost. "You must find that old badger right away."

"What should I say to her? She seems so grumpy."

"Tell her the truth. It's usually the best choice," Carl the Third advised.

I left Carl in my chamber. When I came downstairs, there was Zeddicus, waiting for me with a list of chores. It was dusk by the time I had cleaned and cooked and chopped wood for the fire.

Twice, when Zeddicus thought I was working too slowly, he tightened the noose around my neck.

"Just as a reminder," he said, eyes glinting.

I rubbed my neck and imagined what might happen if I killed him today. Would his death break the spell? Or would I be left a prisoner forever?

At last, at twilight, I found the badger putting away her spade and trowel.

"Good evening, Magda," I said.

The badger didn't acknowledge me in any way.

"Please, Magda, I need your help," I said. "Please talk to me." I felt tears in my eyes, and my voice trembled. "We're both prisoners here..." I could not go on for fear of crying in desperation.

"I—I must get away," I stammered. "Santer has taken over my home, and plans to marry my sister—that is, if she's still alive."

Slowly, Magda turned around, and pointed a claw at my chest.

For the first time since I'd arrived at the Towers, Magda looked directly into my eyes. If I'd been on the verge of tears before, the sorrow in her eyes was my undoing. She waited while I wiped my cheeks with my palms.

"I had a dream," I said. "A woman with the head of a wolf stepped through a ring of fire. She told me to ask you, but she didn't tell me the question. That's all she said, 'Ask the badger.'"

Magda inclined her head slightly, and waited.

"Can you help me escape from this place?" I asked. "Do you know how to break the chaining spell?"

When Magda finally spoke, her voice was soft, not low and growly as I'd expected.

108

"Make a ring of willow bark, big enough to step through," Magda told me. "Weave into the ring strands of the old man's hair. At midnight, at the dark of the moon, set it alight where the barrier ends. Then step through. Be sure to tie up the dogs and feed them well. If they bark and he wakens, he'll send them after you."

"Will you come with me?" I asked. Her sadness hurt my heart.

"Perhaps," she said, looking around at the garden. "Perhaps."

"How can I thank you?" I said.

Magda just turned away, shaking her head. She stumped slowly down the path and into her hollow tree.

The moon was waning.

I had only a few days to prepare the willow ring. There were many willow trees within reach on the Towers land. It was not difficult to gather branches and hide them behind the woodpile.

Little by little, I stripped the branches and brought the bark up to my chamber, hidden under my tunic. That part was easy. But I could not think of a way to collect strands of Zeddicus's hair. His chamber was closed to me.

I swept all the corners of the Towers, finding nothing. Finally, on washday, I searched through his garments and was rewarded with five, long white hairs.

As I wove the willow bark into a ring, I blessed old Mata Jira for teaching me how to make baskets.

The panther in the dungeon was never far from my mind.

Would Zeddicus send it after me? I had to take the chance because Agatha was on her way.

Now my preparations are complete. I finished the willow bark ring last night. Tomorrow night is the dark of the moon.

Here, I will end my journal. I shall put this account into my pack, along with my few belongings.

If Zeddicus should recapture me, or if the panther kills me, Carl the Third will take the tidings to Agatha at Two Rivers. I am leaving the window open for him to fly out at dawn. We shall travel together if I achieve my freedom.

Carl
the Third

Chapter Nineteen
Zeddicus

Agatha waited alone on a rock in the pasture. Her horse grazed nearby. Agatha knew Archer would come, but she suspected that the bird was watching her and waiting. It wouldn't be beyond Archer to let Agatha stew in her own thoughts and worry for a while.

Agatha had a lot to think about. She wanted to stay at Green River for so many reasons—Garret being one of them.

That morning he had helped her saddle the horse, and when she wouldn't let him accompany her, he had said he wouldn't let her go without a kiss.

Another reason she didn't want to leave was the girls: Gwyndar, Tamara, Solvi, and Delia. Their companionship, the entertainments they invented, the fussing over clothes and hair—all this was new to Agatha, and she found it delightful and surprising.

The admiration of Agatha's skill with the mangle, and the family's appreciation were also gratifying. Being the center of attention was a new experience for Agatha. At Hawk Hill, she had always been in Malcolm's shadow. Ah, yes, and then there was Malcolm—the whole purpose of the journey.

Perhaps the most worrisome of all was the panther.

Over the pasture, the sun rose higher.

Agatha waited, brooding. She wanted to stay, but she had to go. She knew Archer would not spare her. The bird was as arrow-straight in her purpose as in her flight.

Finally, the falcon appeared. She sailed over the trees and landed on the rock next to Agatha.

"I hope you've had your fill of picnics and games," Archer said. "We must leave today."

Agatha sighed and stared at her hands.

"What?" Archer exclaimed. "Don't tell me you've given up! Not now that we know where he is!"

Agatha's head jerked up. "We do? How?"

Archer fluffed her breast feathers. "I met the bird who told your Aunt Viola that Malcolm was alive. He's a raven. Rather young for such a mission, but he seems devoted to your brother. Said Malcolm saved his life."

"Archer, wait," Agatha said. "Tell it to me from the beginning, please. What happened after the panther attacked Cam?"

"Well, while you went off to be pampered and dressed up like a pet monkey," Archer said, "I was out looking for clues. I came upon a flock of starlings heading south. Terrible gossips, starlings, but they do get around. They were talking about a raven that had flown down from the north, all the way from beyond Two Rivers. That got my attention. So I asked where I could find him."

"And?" Agatha prodded.

Archer paused to stretch her wings. "The starlings said he was on his way back to the Towers," Archer said. "That is where your brother is held prisoner."

"Malcolm is a prisoner?"

"Yes, according to the raven," Archer said. "The bird's name is Carl, Carl the Third, to be exact. He was prone to frequent digressions of his illustrious ancestry. Something about the ravens guarding a castle gate. It was hard to get him to stay focused."

"Please, Archer, just tell me about Malcolm," Agatha said, twisting her hair.

"Yes, well. Malcolm is a prisoner in the Towers," Archer said, "northwest of the Two Rivers, near a town called Calinia."

"Who is his keeper?"

"Ah, that is the key," said Archer. "The keeper is an old warlock named Zeddicus. He has some connection to Santer, but the raven couldn't recall the details." Archer paused to watch a pair of mourning doves skim over the pasture.

"How soon can we leave?" Archer asked.

Agatha closed her eyes. "Lord Harold and his people aren't going to let me go alone. It's not like Hawk Hill. Even if I could sneak out to the stable tonight, the grooms would hear me. They sleep above the stalls."

"Then you cannot go back," Archer said. "Do you have your mangle and your knife?"

"Yes, but—" Agatha began. She cast longing eyes toward the great house. "I suppose you're right. There is no other way."

Agatha mounted the horse. Archer flew up onto Agatha's arm and settled her feathers. Agatha kicked the horse to a canter. They would be long into the hills before Garret realized that Agatha was not coming back.

Chapter Twenty

The Towers

Agatha awakened when the birds began their morning chorus. Feeling stiff and cold, she brushed pine needles from her tunic. Even though she was hungry, Agatha refused to share Archer's meal of grackle. She remained thirsty, too, as the water in her skin bag was bad.

"I suppose it doesn't matter whether we travel by day or night?" she said to Archer, as she used her fingers to take some of the tangles out of her hair. "And Malcolm is close by," Agatha added. "My heart tells me so."

Archer turned her head to take in a view of their surroundings.

"Perhaps you are right," the gyrfalcon said. "If the panther is after you, it could attack in the dark or light. I can see quite a distance from above. Let's move on now."

For three days, they traveled north with no sign of the panther.

Following the Green River along the foothills of the Peaks, they made their way to the town of Calinia.

When Agatha asked for directions, the townsfolk told her how to find the Towers, and the warlock, Zeddicus.

"Beware of Old Man Zeddicus," one shopkeeper warned Agatha. "He's got powers, and he's not to be trusted."

Not far outside of Calinia, Agatha could see three stone turrets above the trees. Her heart began to beat fast.

"Look! The Towers!" Agatha said. "Malcolm is there. I can feel it."

"*May* be there," Archer said. "Let me scout around."

Agatha tossed the falcon into the air and watched as the bird approached the Towers.

Archer circled once around, and then she didn't reappear.

Agatha waited under the trees. She had to force herself to stay still. For the first time in three years, she felt again the pull in her chest that told her Malcolm was near. She knew he had not yet escaped.

At last, Archer returned.

"I found the raven sunning himself on Malcolm's window ledge," Archer said. "He tells me that Malcolm has

found a way to escape. And tonight is the right time to break the spell that holds him."

Agatha's eyes widened. She clasped her hands together to stop them from shaking.

Archer ruffled her feathers and stretched out her wings. "I'm hungry," she said. "Let's go back into the forest. You can find some of that plant stuff you eat, and I'll get us some meat."

"All right," Agatha said. "But please, Archer, could it be a pigeon? The poor songbirds are all bones, and the grackles are simply inedible."

Leading the horse, Agatha followed Archer deeper into the woods. She picked some berries, but she was too anxious to eat much. Meals had been skimpy and irregular since they left Green River. Lord Harold's manse, with its sumptuous banquets, seemed like a dream of long ago. Agatha felt as if she'd been living on half-cooked fish, berries, and cattail roots for her whole life.

Agatha sat down with her back against an oak tree, and let her mind drift. First to Malcolm. Then to Garret. And finally, to Aunt Viola and Sloane. These were the people who mattered to her. The panther invaded her thoughts with ominous frequency. Agatha had not seen even a shadow of a beast as they journeyed north to the Towers.

Archer, having eaten, flew off again to observe the Towers. Agatha waited under the oak, making designs with acorns in the dirt. When Archer finally returned, the falcon had much to report.

"I saw Malcolm," Archer said. "He was chopping wood in the yard. He's grown to man-size. There are two big dogs lolling about under a pear tree. And there's a bent-over old badger working in the garden."

"And did you see the warlock?" Agatha asked.

"Yes, he stepped out of the door to tell Malcolm he wasn't working fast enough. Then he did something with his fingers and Malcolm seemed to choke."

"What about the panther? Did you see it?" Agatha's hands were balled up in fists.

"No sign or shadow."

Agatha twisted her hair. "It is agony being so close and having to wait."

"Yes, you humans can be impatient creatures," Archer said. "I'm going to talk to the raven."

"I wish I could go with you," Agatha said with a sigh, watching the falcon take flight. She laid her head on her folded arms, then closed her eyes.

A sharp pain in her arm woke her.

Archer was nipping Agatha with her beak.

"Ouch! Stop!" Agatha cried.

"Wake up and pay attention!" Archer said. "The raven tells me that the panther is locked in the Towers' dungeon. The beast is under the warlock's control."

Agatha's face paled. "I still have my mangle. Maybe I can take it down again, even if I can't kill it."

"Yes, it is well to be prepared," said Archer. "The sun is setting now. Soon it will be too dark for me to help you."

The falcon went to settle herself on a high limb near the Towers' yard.

Agatha crept closer, staying hidden among the shadows. She studied the Towers, and saw a small light in the tallest of the turrets, the one with all the windows. A shadow figure moved about.

Was it Malcolm?

Or was it the warlock?

She could not tell. It was painful to be so close to her brother and unable to reach out to him. Even worse was the possibility that the panther would kill one of them first.

After hours of waiting, Agatha heard small sounds coming from the yard. The dark shapes of the three towers, like menacing giants, loomed above her. From her hiding place, Agatha detected a figure moving about, carrying something large.

Agatha could feel that it was Malcolm. She wanted to call out to him, to let him know she was there, but she dared not. She had to stay hidden, and trust that Malcolm would break the spell that kept him prisoner.

Malcolm set down his burden at the very edge of the yard—a large woven circle of basketry. Using several sticks, he propped it upright. He threw a large pack into the trees that bordered the yard, beyond the woven wreath. Then Agatha heard him muttering. Sparks suddenly flew out from

his fingers. The basket ring began to smoke, then the branches caught fire. Soon the whole ring was burning.

In its light, Agatha could see her brother waiting and watching the flames.

Wrapping himself tightly in his cloak, Malcolm jumped through the burning circle. At the same moment, the warlock appeared in the doorway of the second tower, with the panther at his side.

"Go get him!" the warlock shouted. "Finish him off!"

Agatha stood ready with her mangle.

Before she could set it swinging, another creature leapt forward and began grappling with the panther. It was Magda, the old badger. The two creatures rolled together, in and out of the firelight.

Agatha stepped closer, but the combatants were too tightly entwined for her to throw her weapon accurately.

Malcolm, now safely on the other side of the barrier, hesitated. The badger pushed and pulled the big cat toward the burning circle. The panther was so intent on its attacker that it rolled into the flames before it could avoid the blaze. Its black fur caught fire like dry kindling. The cat let out a long, furious howl, and disappeared in a cloud of sulfurous, oily smoke.

Bloody and burned, Magda the badger lay on the ground outside the smoldering circle.

Agatha stepped out from the shadows.

"Agatha?" Malcolm said.

Agatha could not speak. She only nodded.

Brother and sister gazed at each other for a long moment. Then they fell into each other's arms. But the warlock interrupted the reunion.

In a rage, Zeddicus ran toward them, shouting, "Foul fiend! You will not live another day!"

Malcolm spread his fingers as the warlock came close, and sent showers of sparks onto Zeddicus's robe. The warlock's hair and robe erupted in flames.

Zeddicus shrieked and threw himself to the ground. He beat wildly at the flames on his head, and rolled back and forth to extinguish the burning cloth. Then he collapsed, motionless in a smoking heap.

On the ground, outside the charred wreath, Magda groaned in pain.

Together, Agatha and Malcolm knelt beside the brave beast.

The badger stirred and opened her eyes.

"If you can deliver me to my cousins who live near the river," Magda gasped, "they will care for me." Then she

closed her eyes again, breathing so lightly that Agatha feared she had died. Malcolm felt for her pulse.

"Right," Malcolm said. "She's still alive. We'll do as she asks."

"I have a horse," said Agatha. "Help me carry her."

The twins' eyes met in such an exchange of joy that the air around them seemed to vibrate and ring.

Together, Agatha and Malcolm lifted the wounded badger and made their way to the horse.

It was a day's slow walking to reach the pasture near Green River. Agatha and Malcolm took turns riding behind Magda. Both twins knew that they were going in the opposite direction from their destination of the Two Rivers' crossing, but neither mentioned it. The old badger was obviously in great pain. But like most beasts, even the talking ones, she didn't complain.

On the way, Agatha and Malcolm shared the events of the last three years. For Agatha, hearing the account of her parents' murder was hardest of all. Together they wept for the loss of their mother and father.

"So it was you who sent the wolf that saved me?" Agatha said, on hearing how Malcolm taught himself spells from the warlock's books. She hugged him again. "You're so big! I almost didn't recognize you!"

Around midday, Archer and Carl the Third joined them. The two birds scouted ahead in shifts. When Archer was out flying, she spied the badgers and their sett—a series of hollows in a field near the riverbank.

In the early evening, they delivered Magda into her relatives' care. The family of badgers was one of the only clans of talking badgers left in the country.

Two badgers carried Magda away into a tunnel to treat her injuries. Magda's sister took them to another entrance.

"How big is this place?" Malcolm asked.

"Oh, our sett is centuries old," Magda's sister answered. "Our family has lived here for years and years. Over time, we badgers have added on so many tunnels and chambers that it's like an underground town."

Magda's sister gave Malcolm and Agatha some cooked roots to eat. She showed them into a chamber where they could rest. It smelled strongly of badger.

Malcolm fell asleep right away, but Agatha lay awake for a while. Her thoughts were jumping from fear and excitement. She kept wondering what Santer and the warlock Zeddicus might do now, and how she and Malcolm would reclaim Hawk Hill.

Malcolm woke her so she could hear Archer's report.

"No one is following you yet," Archer told them. "The warlock is badly burned and has taken to his bed."

In the morning, as they prepared to leave, Magda's sister returned Agatha's cloak. Somehow she'd managed to clean it during the time they'd slept.

"Off you go now," she said. "Follow the stream to the river road. The ford is to the south. You should get there by dusk."

"Your sister Magda saved my life," Malcolm told her. "If you ever have need of help, send for me."

They bid farewell and turned east toward Two Rivers. The journey took two days, but to Malcolm and Agatha, time was insignificant because they were together again.

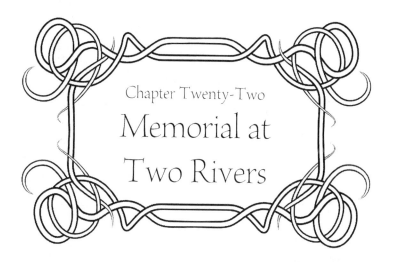

Chapter Twenty-Two

Memorial at Two Rivers

On the morning of the third day, Agatha, Malcolm, and the birds arrived at Two Rivers. The town itself was on the other side of the conjunction of Green River and the River Banneck. Their arrival at the place of their parents' deaths was a somber event.

"I wonder if their bodies were ever found?" Agatha said.

"I know, I've wondered, too," Malcolm said. "I wanted to go back and look for them, but I was too afraid Santer would catch me."

They stared at the water for a long time without speaking.

"How shall we destroy him?" Agatha asks.

"We'll find a way," Malcolm said. "He will pay for what he's done."

They were standing side by side on the bank of the River Banneck. The brown water spun by in gentle curls and hills.

"Three years ago, when I was here with our parents, the river was in flood," Malcolm told Agatha. "Whole trees went by with their roots sticking up like arms. The water was brown and the waves smashed on the banks. The noise was so loud that I couldn't hear anything from the raft that our parents and Santer were on. I could see their mouths moving, but that was all. And then Santer tipped Mother overboard, and Oscar told me to flee." Malcolm heaved a long sigh. "I'll never forget it."

They stood on the dock used for boarding the raft, which on that day was moored on the other side of the river.

Agatha thought about their parents, trying to recall how they looked and the sound of their voices. "I feel terrible that I can barely bring their faces to mind," she said.

"I know," Malcolm agreed. "It's the same for me."

"I can't believe that only three years have passed since our parents drowned here," Agatha said. "It seems like centuries."

"Let's make a memorial for them," Malcolm proposed.

They decided to build a cairn with the river rocks.

It took most of the day to carry and place the rocks. Finally, the twins set the capstone on top of the cairn.

Agatha picked out a flat piece of shale to put at the base of the memorial. All she could find to write with was a charcoal stick taken from the cold campfire. She wrote:

Lord Durwin and Lady Merle
of Hawk Hill Manse
Beloved Parents

"I know the rain will wash the words away," she said to her brother, "but I feel better for writing them."

Malcolm and Agatha stood together and contemplated the stack of rocks.

"You should have added 'foully murdered,' Malcolm said.

"There wasn't room for more words on the slate," Agatha replied.

"The words may wash away," Malcolm said, "but the cairn will last for ages."

Malcolm took Agatha's hand in his.

"We'll take back Hawk Hill," Malcolm said. "I don't know how yet, but we will."

"One thing I do know," Agatha said. "Now that we are together, anything is possible."

Part Two

Chapter Twenty-Three
The Dwarf at the Inn

Malcolm and Agatha had just finished constructing the memorial to their parents when Archer swooped down from above. She landed on the top of the cairn.

"This is a fitting tribute to your good parents," Archer said from atop the stones. "They were fine, generous people. You've built it well. Now it's time to return to Hawk Hill."

They rinsed their hands in the water, stopping often to gaze at the stack of flat river stones with satisfaction.

"I feel horribly grimy and sweaty," Agatha said to Malcolm. For days she had longed for a hot bath, and clean hair and clothes. Sometimes, during the nights on the way to the Towers, she had even dreamt of a tub of hot water and scented soap.

"You'll have to wait to have a decent wash," said

Malcolm. "Archer's right. It's past time we started for home." He shaded his eyes, scanning the riverbank. "Where is Carl?"

"Carl is over there." Agatha pointed to the raven, who was at the river's edge, making a tiny cairn of his own with sparkling pebbles. "Is Carl always this silly?" she asked Malcolm.

"He has his moments of foolishness," Malcolm answered, "but he's a loyal friend."

Malcolm untied the horse from the tree branch beside the riverbank. Agatha picked up Malcolm's pack, staggering for a moment under its weight.

"What have you got in here?" Agatha asked. She could barely heave the sack behind the saddle, where she secured it with rope.

"Oh, I lifted a few books from Zeddicus's library," Malcolm said. "I've been studying." He grinned. "I also took a few gold tiffins from his treasure box. I figured he owed me a little for all my months of work."

"You have money?" Agatha said. "We could move a lot faster with—"

"Another horse?" Malcolm finished. He always seemed to know what she was thinking.

Agatha still couldn't believe that they were together

again. They talked endlessly about the past and what lay ahead as they walked beside the horse, while the birds kept in front of them in the trees. Heading south on the river road, they maintained a watchful eye on the woods. The panther may have fizzled into smoke, but they feared that the warlock might conjure another beast to harm them.

The following evening, they passed by a village. Agatha stayed with the birds and the horse while Malcolm went to see where he might buy another mount.

When he returned, he said, "There's an inn with a stable just on the other side of the village. The hostler might have a horse to sell us."

"An inn?" Agatha said. "We haven't had a proper meal for days. I'm tired of eating the birds Archer catches. All those little bones, and they burn so easily."

"You two are ungrateful beggars," said Archer. "From now on, you can catch your own dinner."

"Then let's stay at the inn tonight," said Malcolm.

Archer objected. "Staying at the inn is a bad idea," she warned. "Buy the horse, but move on in haste."

"Please," Agatha begged. "Just for one night?"

"One night," Malcolm agreed.

From the hostler, Malcolm purchased a solid, cooperative mare. She was not much to look at, being dun-

colored and rather dusty, but her manners were pleasant. He stabled both horses and Agatha made sure the birds were safely hidden for the night.

Archer continued to be unhappy about the inn.

"This place could be dangerous," she said before Agatha left her. "You don't know who may be after you."

With their belongings locked in an upstairs chamber, Malcolm and Agatha went downstairs to dine. The inn's common room was crowded and noisy. They took seats at the end of a long table. A pink-faced serving girl brought bowls of stew, and mugs of cider.

"This stew is more grease than meat," said Malcolm, "and the cider is watery."

"I don't care," Agatha told him. "I'm grateful for the change. And it feels glorious to be clean. I even washed my hair."

Off in a dark corner sat a stout, hairy man with flinty, small eyes.

Agatha could feel those eyes on her as she ate.

"That man in the corner won't leave off staring at me," she said to Malcolm. "It's giving me the shivers."

Malcolm checked over his shoulder and stiffened.

"Agatha, there's something under his table," he said. "I just saw the hairy fellow kick it."

"Is it a dog?" Agatha asked.

"No," Malcolm said, after observing a bit. "It's a child."

They sipped a second mug of cider as they waited for the food ordered for the next day's journey. After a while, the man stood and dropped some coins on the table. Leaning down, he yanked on the child's arm.

The boy who crawled out from under the table couldn't have been older than eleven. His face was smeared with dirt and tracked by tears. He was a miserable wretch, half-starved and dressed in rags.

"He looks almost as bad as Rami did when I found her in the forest," Agatha said.

As the man and boy made their way across the common room, the diners turned and watched, but no one interfered. Even though the boy was obviously being mistreated, people seemed to draw away in fear. Mounting the staircase closest to their table, the man pushed the child ahead of him. When the boy tripped, the fellow booted him back to his feet.

Agatha caught sight of the earring dangling from the man's ear. It was a silver circle with a clear crystal set in the center. Malcolm saw it, too.

"That earring means he's a full-blooded dwarf," Malcolm said. "He's probably taking the boy to work in the forges under the mountain."

"I can't bear the thought," Agatha said. "We have to rescue him."

Malcolm laughed at her.

"Wasn't saving one child enough for you?" he said. "We have more pressing tasks."

"How can you be so heartless?" Agatha cried. "That boy will surely die in the mines. Look at him! He's half-dead already. We have two horses. We can bring him with us."

"And move twice as slowly and be more conspicuous," Malcolm said. "And let Santer entrench himself even further on our lands." Malcolm shook his head. "No, sister dear, we are not getting involved."

"Could you find a sleeping spell?" Agatha asked Malcolm, ignoring his protests. "Or a spell to bind the dwarf to a chair?"

"I only have the sparks," Malcolm said. "Magic requires study and practice. It's foolish to take chances with untried spells."

"Then we may have to grab the boy and run," she said.

"Run from a dwarf? Good luck with that," Malcolm sneered.

Agatha ignored that comment, too.

The serving maid brought their packet of food. Malcolm put it inside his carry bag.

Agatha could see that Malcolm wasn't going to help, so she decided to hatch a plan of her own.

As they stood up to go to their sleeping quarters, the dwarf returned alone to the common room, and ordered a tankard of ale. Malcolm went on upstairs, but Agatha stayed for a while in the shadow of the stairway and watched. The dwarf quickly finished all the ale, and ordered another. His movements showed that he was getting sloppy from the drink. The dwarf's drunkenness might help her plan, if only she could come up with one.

In their room, Malcolm was already asleep. Even though it was a frosty night, he'd left the window open, as they'd promised the birds they would. Malcolm had hung his kerchief on the casement latch, to signal the spot to Archer and Carl.

Agatha lay awake trying to come up with a way to free the boy. He was locked in a room somewhere along the hall, quite nearby. Breaking into his room would cause too much of a stir. If they knew which chamber was his, they might climb up to his window from outside. Agatha could almost feel his misery seeping through the walls, but she could not devise a plan. Eventually, she slept.

Chapter Twenty-Four

Rats

Archer and Carl woke them at first light.

"It's past time to move on," Archer said, always the one to prod. "You should have been ready by now."

Carl flew onto the foot of the bed where he tweaked Malcolm's toes. Then he started fiddling with something shiny, the way he often did. He was always on the lookout for objects that glittered.

"What's that you've got there, Carl?" Malcolm asked.

"Oh, just something I found in the yard," Carl answered.

Agatha looked closer.

"It's a key," she said. "It looks like one of the chamber keys. Where did you get this, Carl?"

"The hairy man dropped it on his way to the privy," Carl said. "Pretty, isn't it?"

Agatha snatched the key out of Carl's beak. "You brilliant bird!" she cried.

"No, Agatha!" Malcolm said. He tried to grab the key from her. "Bad idea."

Agatha pulled away. Leaning far out the window, she saw the drunken dwarf passed out on a bench.

"The timing is perfect," she said. "Are you going to help me or not?"

Malcolm only shook his head, but he slung his carry bag over his shoulder and followed her into the hallway.

After a few tries, they did find the right lock. The boy was huddled in a corner on the floor when they entered.

"Come with us," Agatha whispered. "We'll keep you safe."

She held out her hand to help him up, but he shrank back into the corner.

"Come on, hurry!" Agatha told him. "The dwarf is passed out in the stable yard." She reached out to him again. He cowered further against the wall.

"I've got an idea," said Malcolm.

He pulled a bun from the packet of food in his carry bag. Breaking off a bit, he held it out to the boy.

"You must be hungry," Malcolm said. "Come with us and I'll give you the rest."

The boy examined Malcolm and the piece of bread. He crawled crab-like across the floor and snatched the bread from Malcolm's fingers. Stuffing it into his mouth, he held out his hand for more.

"I'll give it to you when we get to the stable," Malcolm told him. "Agatha, go ask the hostler to ready the horses."

Agatha collected her belongings and tiptoed down the narrow back staircase. Malcolm and the child followed soon after. At the stable, she bundled the boy into her shawl and set him in front of Malcolm on the dun horse.

Keeping the pace at a steady trot, they put several miles between the village and themselves before they stopped to eat. Carl and Archer joined them there.

Archer was furious.

"What is this penchant you have for picking up stray children?" Archer said. "Are you planning to start an orphanage? Do you imagine that the dwarf won't follow you? You've increased your danger three-fold, and you've put the boy in danger, too!"

Agatha and Malcolm had never seen Archer so angry. Malcolm nodded in agreement with the gyrfalcon. To his credit, he kept silent. But Archer enchanted the boy.

"Blimey, that bird can really talk!" he said, after he'd eaten most of the food.

The boy's name was Odell. His parents had a farm up by Oxdenn Town. Archer was the first to notice Odell's skin.

"That boy is as green as Rami," she said. "He's probably another changeling from the Grassmen."

It was true. When he'd cleaned up a bit, Odell had the same greenish skin, and his hair was as pale as dandelion fluff.

"My mother told me she lost her real baby boy to the Grassmen," Odell said. "But she always said she loved me as her own." He clenched his jaw so he wouldn't cry. "I know I'm a half-breed, but I'm still a good worker on the farm."

"We're going to a farm, too," Agatha said.

There wasn't any point in telling Odell the whole story about Santer and scaring him more. He was already so nervous, checking for the dwarf all the time, and startling at every sharp sound.

The three rode many miles all that day and into the night. Beside the river, they stopped and made camp. Malcolm caught fish for dinner.

All were bedded down and asleep by the fire when Odell woke up screaming.

"Rats!" he shrieked. "Rats!"

The rats came swarming toward them from the riverbank, a dozen rodents as big as barn cats. Their evil,

glittery eyes reflected the firelight. The beasts were on top of them before they could unwrap themselves from their cloaks. Agatha's mangle was out of reach in the saddlebag, so she took a burning stick from the fire to fend them off. Odell did the same.

One of the rodents bit Agatha's boot so hard that it broke through the leather. Odell kept screaming. Malcolm had his knife out, slashing at the awful sleek bodies with their scaly tails. They could hear the rats' teeth clicking.

"Do something, Malcolm!" Agatha shouted. "Throw sparks at them!"

Malcolm muttered the words of the spell. He flicked his fingers toward the rats. Sparks rained onto their backs. The air smelled of burning fur.

Malcolm kept showering sparks. The rats snarled and hissed at him, but they started to back down toward the water.

Odell and Agatha picked up rocks. They added a barrage of stones to Malcolm's sparks. The rats disappeared into the black water.

"We only managed to kill two," Malcolm said as he booted the bodies into the river.

Odell suffered several bites on his feet and ankles. Agatha cleaned and dressed his wounds as best she could. By the time she'd finished, it was dawn.

When they were out of Odell's hearing, Malcolm and Agatha had a whispered conversation.

"Those rats were sent by magic," Malcolm said. "Santer and Zeddicus know where we are."

"What should we do?" Agatha asked.

"Ride for home as fast as we can," Malcolm said. "No more inns. No more children," he added. "I wish I had time to study Zeddicus's books."

Agatha shuddered, thinking of the rats, and the warlocks' attempt to harm them. What might they try next?

Rats

All three were wary and watchful as they rode southward. With Archer's guidance from above, they traveled on the side roads and camped in the woods. Agatha kept expecting Archer to spot someone pursuing them, but she never did.

Someone was following Odell. The follower kept himself well hidden among the trees.

A day after the rats attacked, they had stopped by a stream for a midday meal when Odell gave a shout.

"There's a man behind that tree!" He pointed at a sturdy maple a few yards away. "I saw him peeking out at us. And I think he's green."

Malcolm jumped up. "Oh, no, not Grassmen!"

The fellow must have heard Odell shout because he stepped out from behind the tree.

"Yes, yes, that is right, little manikin," said the Grassman, coming toward them. "I be a Grassman, and I be taking back my property."

"Keep your distance!" Malcolm shouted at him. "Don't let him get near you!" he yelled to Odell and Agatha. "He's got that—"

Malcolm was too late. The Grassman moved like the wind. He tossed green dust all over them, and Carl, too.

Violent sneezes shook everyone.

The Grassman clapped his hands and shouted gleefully, "The sneezie powder! The sneezie powder be Grassman's power!"

"Go to the stream," Malcolm called out to Agatha and Odell.

Agatha couldn't see anyone, for her eyes were swollen, but she heard the explosive noises they were all making. She felt her way to the stream and bumped into Malcolm doing the same. They rinsed their eyes and dunked their heads in the water.

Agatha lay on the rocks by the stream, wet and sick and exhausted. When she could open her eyes, she saw Malcolm, drenched and limp, lying on the ground nearby.

Poor Carl, who had been talking with Odell, received the worst of the sneezie powder. Every time he sneezed, his feathers blew up like a puffball.

At first they didn't realize the trouble they were in.

Agatha tried to pull herself onto her elbows. Her wrists and legs were bound.

The Grassman knelt over Odell, fiddling with something.

"What are you doing?" Agatha whispered. Her throat was raw, so even that small effort to speak caused her pain.

The Grassman turned around. He was about the same size as Odell, green as a spring leaf, with a long thin nose and a skimpy green beard.

"I be the Grassman Whipstem," he said. "And I be taking this manikin to Liriope."

Liriope was the center of the Grassian country, where the queen had her court.

Malcolm tried to stand up, but the Grassman had bound his wrists and ankles also. Had his legs been free, Malcolm could have tackled the small man from behind. He was so much taller that it seemed an easy thing to do. But now it was a challenge for him just to get to his feet.

"Why are we bound? We've done you no harm," Agatha said.

149

"Oooh, but those be false words," Whipstem said. He shook his finger in her face. "You be taking my property from the Dwarfman Ferg at the inn."

"Your property? Odell is not your property," Agatha said.

"Oooh, yes, he do be so," said Whipstem. "See you this?"

The Grassman, who proved to be surprisingly strong, dragged Odell to where Malcolm and Agatha were sitting. He took Odell by the hair and yanked his head forward. With one skinny green finger, Whipstem pointed to a small dark spot on the back of Odell's neck.

"See this, manikin and ladykin?" he said. "This be a slavey beetle. Myself, the Grassman Whipstem, be putting it there. This little manikin be mine."

"And what will you do with him at Liriope?" Malcolm asked.

"I be taking him back to Ferg," Whipstem answered.

Malcolm and Agatha exchanged a look. Both were thinking about how much trouble they'd taken to save Odell from Ferg. Now it seemed that Odell might end up slaving in the dwarves' mine after all.

"And what about us?" Agatha asked.

"You be staying here," said Whipstem.

The Grassman hauled Odell to his feet. With an amazing show of strength for such a small person, he heaved the boy onto Agatha's horse. Then he picked up Carl, who was still sneezing in spurts on the ground. He stuffed the raven into a sack.

"Wait!" Malcolm shouted. "What are you doing? Carl isn't yours!"

"I be taking this birdie to the Queen," Whipstem answered. "She be liking a talking beastie."

Placing the sack with Carl in front of the saddle, Whipstem mounted the new dun horse. He slapped the reins and off they went through the trees. Once again, Malcolm and Agatha would be traveling on foot.

Malcolm inched his way closer to his sister. "Can you untie this cord?" he asked.

She wriggled around until her fingers reached his bound wrists. She picked at the knots. After a bit, she sighed.

"I can't get a purchase," Agatha said. "And I can barely see. My eyes and nose are burning still."

As they sat back to back, too worn out to think of another plan, Archer dropped down from the branches above. She landed on Agatha's knee.

"First it's rats, then it's Grassmen," Archer grumbled. "I told you that boy would be trouble, but no, you had to save

another child. And now Carl is going to be put in a cage so the Grassian queen can hear him talk. If he survives."

Neither Agatha nor Malcolm had the energy to argue with the gyrfalcon. She glared at Malcolm and then at Agatha with her sharp eyes. Agatha felt as ignorant and small as a worm.

"I should leave you both here to find your own way out of this mess," Archer muttered.

She hopped off Agatha's knee, then walked around behind her and began to slice at Agatha's bindings with her sharp beak.

When their hands and legs were untied and they'd recovered somewhat from the sneezing powder, Agatha and Malcolm held a counsel with Archer.

"Archer, I know you were against rescuing Odell," Malcolm said, "but I think you'll agree that we have to go after Carl."

"If that raven had been in a tree like any self-respecting bird, he wouldn't be on his way to Liriope," Archer said with disdain. "However, I suppose we must make an effort to fetch him back."

Chapter Twenty-Six

Cocooned

Malcolm and Agatha glanced at each other and held their breath, wondering if Archer would offer her help.

Archer sighed. "And I suppose you want me to track Whipstem from the air."

"Oh, would you, Archer?" Agatha said. "Just to see how far they've traveled."

Both Malcolm and Agatha were afraid of demanding more of Archer, after she'd been so gracious to free them. But without a protest, Archer spread her wings and flew after the Grassman.

When the gyrfalcon came back from tracking Whipstem, she said, "He's riding northeast toward Liriope. You can't possibly catch up on foot."

"What choice do we have?" Agatha said.

Malcolm and Agatha were quite done in from the sneeze attack, but they followed the trail of the horses until exhaustion overtook them. They had come to a part of the forest that was dense with vines. The branches of the trees dripped with a strange gray moss that made the place look ghostly.

"I can't go any further," Malcolm said when they stopped to drink at a stream at sunset. "We might as well stay here for the night."

Agatha was happy to agree.

Archer was impatient.

"I shall spend the night near Carl and come back to you tomorrow," she said, and flew away.

Malcolm had a bit of food left in his carry bag. It wasn't much, but they were more tired than hungry. They wrapped themselves in their cloaks and lay down. Just before he fell asleep, Malcolm heard a strange sound. It was a sort of clicking and hissing. Too tired to be wary, his brain put the noise to the stream or the wind in the branches, and he fell asleep beside his sister.

Sunlight in her eyes woke Agatha. She started to stretch and found that she couldn't move. To her horror, she discovered that she was tightly wrapped in a cocoon of silk

thread. The creatures responsible were still creeping over her legs, and Malcolm's as well.

Agatha screamed. The fat, white caterpillars merely hissed and clicked their jaws. Agatha's screeching didn't stop their work. The caterpillars kept right on spreading the thread from their mouths. Agatha guessed it was a mouth, but the things on their heads looked more like forks.

"Do you think Zeddicus or Santer set these creatures on us with magic?" Agatha asked Malcolm.

"I think so," he said. "It has the feel of a conjuring."

Neither of them could do anything but roll side to side, and that just made the caterpillars hiss louder. Malcolm and Agatha became more and more uncomfortable. At first, they felt enormously hungry, but as the time passed, and the sun rose higher, the hunger was replaced by thirst.

"Are they going to bind up our heads and suffocate us?" Malcolm said.

"That would be a disgusting way to die," Agatha groaned.

Then Archer flew in carrying a large sack in her talons.

"Here's your silly raven," she said, then dropped the sack and flew into a nearby tree. "And no worse for wear, from the way he's been carrying on," Archer added.

They could hear Carl the Third's muffled voice complaining from inside the sack.

Archer took in their predicament from her perch.

"You two seem to be in a bind," Archer said. She had the nerve to chuckle at her own joke. "Not such a bad idea," she continued. "Maybe it will keep you out of trouble."

"Get me out of here!" Carl squawked.

The sack wiggled violently.

Archer took a few moments to preen her feathers before she flew down onto the sack. Then she ripped the cloth open with her sharp beak and talons.

Carl emerged, blinking in the daylight.

He bowed to Archer in a most gentlemanly way.

"Thank you," he said. "I am forever indebted to you."

Then Carl noticed Agatha and Malcolm with the dozens of caterpillars crawling over their forms.

"A veritable banquet!" Carl exclaimed.

For once, Carl knew exactly what to do. He flew to the top of a tree and cawed loudly in his raven voice. In moments, a flurry of crows descended into the clearing. They picked off all the caterpillars, eating some and flying off to feed their children with the rest.

Carl swallowed one fat grub and clicked his beak. "A little bland, but filling," he said. "Now, how shall we unwrap you two?"

"My dirk is strapped to my ankle," Malcolm said. "If there's some way to cut it loose—?"

All eyes turned to Archer, who had returned to the tree branch.

"What now?" she said. "I thought my part in this charade was finished."

"If you could just cut the knife loose, perhaps Carl could do the rest," Malcolm said.

"I should have stayed in the mews," Archer said, sounding grumpy. Still, she flew down to Malcolm's feet and began tearing at the threads.

Chapter Twenty-Seven

Liriope

"Thith thtuff ith thticky," Archer said, removing threads from her beak with a talon.

Archer didn't give up. She kept on cutting the gooey webbing, a fraction of an inch at a time.

Soon enough, Malcolm's ankle was free, and Carl was able to pull the dirk from its sheath. Carl made several tries before he worked out how to hold the knife firmly in his beak. Malcolm knew that the tiny nicks and scratches Carl put in his skin were a small price to pay for freedom.

The sun was setting by the time Malcolm cut Agatha loose.

After they made a rather unsatisfactory meal of roasted water snails, dandelion greens and wild onions, they assessed the situation.

"I feel awful about Odell and our horses," Malcolm said. "But I'm more unhappy that Whipstem made off with the warlock's books. We may need those to deal with Santer."

They decided to go after the books and Odell. While the sky was still light, the two set off on the trail of the horses.

"I don't care where we sleep tonight," Agatha said. "I just want to get as far away from those caterpillars as possible."

Archer rode on Agatha's arm, and Carl sat on Malcolm's shoulder.

"Do you suppose the Grassmen read?" Agatha asked. "They don't seem the sort."

They had the answer after tramping on for another hour or so. The bag of precious spell books lay in a lump in the middle of their path. Happily for them, Whipstem the Grassman saw no profit in a heavy bag of books.

"What luck!" Malcolm said. "Do you still want to rescue Odell and the horses? We could forget it and just head south."

Agatha gave him a nasty look that spoke louder than any words she might have said.

They took turns carrying the heavy bag until both grew too tired to continue. Malcolm made a fire while Agatha searched the trees for signs of caterpillars.

Archer and Carl woke them at mid-morning.

"Liriope is only a day's walk from here. If you start now, you will surely arrive before dark," Archer said. "Although I still say this is a foolish waste of time."

The first glimpse of Liriope, the Grass People's town, came just before sunset. The late afternoon light turned all the dwellings to golden-green. Malcolm and Agatha stood at the edge of the forest, gazing at the unexpected sight.

Many small domed huts surrounded a few larger buildings shaped like sheaves of wheat. The Grass People bustled among the houses. Even from that distance, their skin and hair were remarkably green.

"The horses are over there," Agatha said, pointing to a field on the right. "How in the world are we going to find Odell?"

In the end, it wasn't that difficult.

Whipstem had tied the boy to an iron bench in front of his hut. They waited until dark, and then the town of Liriope offered up another surprise. The houses began to glow with the greenish-yellow light of fireflies.

"Although my encounters with Grassmen have been horrendous," Malcolm whispered, "I have to admit that the people have built an enchanting town."

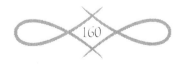

They waited until the Grass folk had retreated into the glowing homes. Then Malcolm and Agatha crept forward, keeping to the shadows. Malcolm used his knife to free Odell while Agatha reclaimed the horses.

They were away before moonrise. Odell seemed weaker than ever. He'd been underfed and mistreated for so long that his mind was confused.

"I want to go home," he moaned. "Take me home."

"You're not safe there, Odell," Agatha said. "You'll be better off at Sloane's farm."

They traveled south through the night, and when daylight came, Agatha used her mangle to take down two rabbits that they roasted over a fire. Odell was so hungry that he ate most of one by himself.

After the meal, he seemed to revive and come to his senses. He knelt by Agatha's side, putting a pale hand on her arm.

"Can you get this thing—this slavey beetle—off my neck?" Odell tipped his head forward and pushed the hair away.

"I can try," she said.

Leaning close, Agatha ran a finger over the black beetle buried in his skin.

"It seems to have dug itself in quite deep," she said. "I may have to use a knife."

"Do whatever you must to take it out," Odell said.

When the slavey beetle was finally removed, Odell had a small but deep hole in his neck.

"It's as if it were growing roots," Agatha said. She held out her hand with the slavey beetle on her palm.

"It looks more like a rooting seed than an insect," Malcolm said.

Agatha crushed it thoroughly with a rock.

"I'll put a little of Sloane's salve on the wound," she said to Odell, "and we can bandage your neck with my kerchief."

"Thank you, sister Agatha, for all your kindness," Odell said. "And you, too, brother Malcolm."

All that day, they hurried the horses as fast as they dared. Archer flew above and reported that she saw no pursuers. They only slept for a few short hours, but when Malcolm and Agatha woke at dawn, Odell and one of the horses were gone.

"I'm sure he's on his way home," Agatha said. "I hope he arrives safely."

"We've already spent precious time chasing Odell, going out of our way and eastward to Liriope," said Malcolm.

Once again, brother and sister were reduced to traveling on foot, as their weight together was too much for one horse. They walked for two uneventful days, until they came again to the crossing at Two Rivers.

Both fell into a dark mood as they pulled the raft to the western bank. Agatha watched their parents' cairn recede in the morning mist, and held Malcolm's hand.

They stopped on the west side to refresh themselves. Agatha stared at the water flowing along, and gave a deep sigh.

"What is it?" Malcolm asked. "Are you thinking of our parents?"

"Always," she answered as she studied her grimy fingernails. "But it's not that. I don't want to seem shallow, but I'm tired of being filthy. I'm tired of eating snails and undercooked fish. Most of all, I want to wash my hair."

"Again?" Malcolm said. "We are not stopping at an inn."

"No, that would be foolish," Agatha agreed. "Would you be willing to give me an hour to wash at the river?" she asked. "I promise I'll be quick."

"You go ahead," Malcolm said. "Take Carl with you. I'll make a fire and catch some fish. I promise to cook them well."

With a much-improved mood, Agatha hurried off to the riverbank with Carl.

Agatha was standing up to her knees in water, rinsing her hair, when she heard a noise that sounded like the barking of an owl mixed with the shriek of a woman. Then something huge and dark lunged out of the water and grabbed her leg in its teeth.

Carl went flapping and squawking for Malcolm.

"Help!" he called. "It's got Agatha! Hurry!"

Chapter Twenty-Eight

Bunyip

Agatha tried to roll away from the creature, but it had her leg in its jaws. The pain was horrible. She knew she was going to be eaten or drown. She grabbed onto a tree root as the monster tried to pull her deeper into the river.

Agatha had no clear memory of the next events. It was only a blur of pain and mud and lots of splashing. She was screaming, and she heard voices, but then she fainted.

Later, Malcolm told her what had happened next.

When Carl came cawing for help, Malcolm snatched up Agatha's mangle. He ran toward the river's edge. A creature the size of a small bear was dragging Agatha into the water. Malcolm raised the mangle and tried to sight a clear shot.

Agatha was dressed only in her undershirt, wrestling and rolling with the creature. Malcolm caught a glimpse of long

tusks, and wet, black fur. Each time he raised the mangle to throw it, Agatha got in the way.

Finally, the creature raised its head and Malcolm loosed the mangle. At the same instant that the mangle wrapped itself around the beast's neck, an arrow swished close to Malcolm's ear and plunged into the creature. Again the bowstring twanged, and another arrow entered the creature's chest. The monster snarled and released Agatha, biting at the arrow shafts lodged in its body.

Agatha crawled up the bank, covered in mud and blood.

A youth close to Malcolm's age ran up beside him. He approached the beast, drew his bow, and loosed a third arrow into its heart.

"Good shooting," Malcolm said, coming up beside him.

"And a fine throw from you." The youth kicked the beast with his boot. "It's quite dead."

"What is it?" Malcolm asked, untwisting the mangle from the creature's neck.

"It's a bunyip. They live in the river," the fellow answered. "Most of the time they don't bother anyone, but they're drawn out of the water by magic. Then they get nasty."

The bunyip had flippers, and a tail like a horse. Its tusks were yellow and pointed, and Malcolm could see rows of sharp teeth in its wide mouth.

The youth removed his arrows from the bunyip's body. Then he faced Malcolm with a worried frown.

"The bunyip must have been roused by a conjuror," he said. "Are you a wizard or a warlock?"

"Not at all," Malcolm said. He decided not to mention his small attempts at magic. Only Santer or Zeddicus could have awakened the bunyip. That meant that they were tracking Malcolm and Agatha—again.

The youth offered his hand. "I'm William, of Green River Manse."

"Malcolm of Hawk Hill," Malcolm told him, but before he could properly thank William, Agatha came out of her swoon and started to scream.

"Help me!" she cried. "My leg!"

William and Malcolm ran to her. She was half-raised on an elbow, trying to clean mud away from a deep gash on her thigh. Agatha gasped when she saw the youth's face.

"William!" she exclaimed.

"Tarwyn!" said the youth.

Malcolm looked from William to his sister.

"You know each other?" he asked. "And who is Tarwyn?"

"She's Tarwyn," William said, pointing at Agatha.

"William is the—the cousin of Garret—of Green River Manse," Agatha said, gasping for breath. "I stayed there—as Tarwyn—some time ago."

Then she fainted again.

"My horse is tethered over there," William said, gesturing at a stand of trees. "We'll take her to the Manse."

William's uncle, Lord Harold, and his family were astounded to be hosting Agatha again. She had told Malcolm the story of how she saved young Cam from the panther, but he heard it again in detail at dinner.

When they had done telling Malcolm of his sister's heroism, and the mysterious disappearance of the dead panther, they insisted on hearing his story.

"And you, young sir, pray tell us how you come to be traveling with your sister?" Lord Harold asked.

Afraid to say much, Malcolm merely answered, "I met with my sister in Oxdenn Town."

Those at the table were too polite to press him further, but he did receive some curious glances.

After the meal, Lord Harold stood and put a hand on Malcolm's shoulder.

"Walk with me a bit, young Malcolm," he said.

When they were strolling in the garden, Lord Harold said, "What is your true story, sir? You and your sister are too well-spoken and accomplished to be the children of a falconer. Tell me the truth and perhaps I can be of assistance."

Thinking quickly, Malcolm made up a tale that was part truth and part fiction.

"It is true, sir, that we are not a falconer's children. I was traveling north with my parents when they drowned at the ford of Two Rivers. As it was not far, I continued on to our destination in Oxdenn Town."

"And where in Oxdenn Town were you bound?"

"To Baron Orkney, a friend of my parents," Malcolm replied. "When Agatha had no word of our arrival, she set out after us, there being no one at home to stop her. We met up and now we are on our way back to Hawk Hill."

Malcolm thought it unwise to speak of Santer, or magic, or the dangers that beset them.

Lord Harold turned and put both his hands on Malcolm's shoulders. He studied him with a thoughtful look in his eyes.

"And how do you explain the gyrfalcon?" he asked.

"My sister is fond of the bird," Malcolm said. "Agatha takes Archer everywhere."

"I have a feeling there is more to your story than you are telling," Lord Harold said. "But I see you are unwilling to reveal more. Even so, you and your sister are welcome to stay as long as you wish."

Malcolm thanked Lord Harold for his kindness, and went to check on Agatha.

Lady Rowena and the old nurse had bathed and bandaged her and put her to bed.

"How's the leg?" Malcolm asked.

"It hurts," she said. "But I'm clean. They even washed my hair." She shook her head and made her chestnut hair bounce. "Where are the birds?"

"I left them both up on a rafter in the stable," Malcolm said. "Archer is annoyed at the delay, but Carl is making much of the part he played in saving you."

He had just enough time to fill her in on the tale he'd told Lord Harold when there was a soft knock on the door.

A voice said, "It's Garret. May I come in?"

Agatha flushed pink. Malcolm narrowed his eyes at her.

"Yes, come in," she answered, straightening her tunic with nervous hands.

Lord Harold's son, Garret, stepped into the chamber. He barely spared Malcolm a glance. His eyes were only on Agatha.

"I'll go check on the horse," Malcolm said, but Garret seemed not to hear him.

Malcolm raised his eyebrows, silently asking Agatha if she wanted him to stay. She smiled and shook her head.

Agatha was surprised that her brother had become so fiercely protective, although, given their recent adventures, his concern was probably justified. She felt pulled in two directions: sorry that her twin was worried, and excited to be reunited with Garret.

Chapter Twenty-Nine

The Proposal

For Malcolm and Agatha, staying at Green River Manse was a welcome change from life on the road. It was almost like a dream, after days of camping and eating skimpy meals. Lord Harold and his family provided every comfort, from excellent food to hunting and picnics.

However, in spite of the comfort, all through their stay, Malcolm woke up several times during the night in a fit of worry. What if Santer harmed Lord Harold's family? How would he and Agatha overcome Santer's magical powers?

During the days, while Agatha lay in her chamber, nursing her leg, Malcolm got a taste of life in a house full of wealthy young people.

"If I weren't so worried about the delay and Santer's magic," Malcolm said, "I would find this interlude quite enjoyable."

There were many distractions.

William and Walter were constantly devising games and contests. Since Agatha's previous visit, they had procured mangles. If it weren't raining, Malcolm, William, and Walter spent time practicing with the weapons. The boys also held archery displays and horse races.

The girls at the manse planned many entertainments. Once Agatha was well enough to be carried outdoors, they had picnics on the fine days. In the evenings, the girls arranged concerts. Each of them played an instrument, some better than others. They all sang. The one named Solvi had an exceptional voice.

Garret did not participate in any of his cousins' entertainments. He chose to sit by Agatha's side.

"He follows you everywhere like a loyal hound," Malcolm said in disgust.

Certainly Agatha was not used to such attention. Garret fetched tea or blankets if he thought she were cold. When it was mealtime, he escorted her to the table.

"Every time I want to speak to you in private, he's there," Malcolm grumbled. "The only way to find you alone is early in the morning, before the household is awake."

A week went by with no interference from Santer's magic.

Finally, one day, Agatha's leg had healed enough for her to walk. That same day, Malcolm told the family that he and his sister needed to journey on very soon.

Malcolm's warning of their imminent departure pressured Garret to speak. In the evening, when he helped Agatha to her chamber, Garret asked if he could come with them.

"I'll be an asset to whatever challenges you face on your journey," he said. "I'm a good bowman, and getting better with the mangle." He paused and added, "And I think you like my company as much as I like yours."

Before Agatha could respond, Garret reached for her hand. "And maybe, sometime later when all is well at Hawk Hill, you'll consider an engagement."

Agatha was quite flustered, and begged for a few moments to compose her thoughts.

"Malcolm and I have so much yet ahead of us," she said at last, pressing her hands to her flushed cheeks. "Restoring Hawk Hill Manse is our task alone." Who knew, she thought, if they would triumph over Santer, or fall victim to his evil? "I can't pledge myself to you, Garret. Not yet."

"But—?" he said. "It sounds like you may, perhaps, later on—?"

When her heart had found a slower pace, Agatha said, "As much as I enjoy your company, and admire you, I cannot agree to a betrothal until Malcolm and I have set Hawk Hill Manse to rights." She paused with a regretful smile. "Let us plan to meet again within the year, if all goes well."

Garret frowned at first, and then sighed. "Yes, you're being quite sensible. I suppose that is the reasonable path, however, my heart is greatly disappointed."

Early the next morning, when Malcolm came to check on her, Agatha told him of Garret's proposal.

"Garret wants us to become engaged," she said.

Her brother paled and looked so stricken that she thought he might be ill.

"Oh, so you're going to marry him," Malcolm said in the bitterest of tones, "and let me reclaim Hawk Hill Manse by myself?"

"How could you even think that?" Agatha burst out. "After all I went through to find you? And all we've been through since? You're all the family I have left!" She was so angry that she threw a pillow at his head.

He ducked.

"I hoped that was how you felt, but I was afraid," Malcolm admitted.

"You could have chosen to marry one of Walter's sisters," Agatha teased. "The middle one, Tamara, is beautiful and so sweet. She was flirting with you, in case you didn't notice."

"Oh, I noticed," Malcolm said. "But those girls are like pampered lapdogs. They only have fluff for brains."

"I think we're both too young for marriage," Agatha said. "Besides, we've got Santer to deal with first."

During their stay at Green River, Archer flew out every day to check for danger. After a while she became impatient. Even Carl grew restless.

"Archer came to my window," Agatha told Malcolm. "She heard from a migrating hawk that Zeddicus is healed. Another warlock was visiting him at the Towers."

"Is it Santer?" Malcolm asked.

"The hawk didn't have more information," Agatha said. "But I think we should go. Today, if possible."

"And Garret?"

"He wanted to join us, but I told him no," she answered. "I said that I would send word with Carl when the two of us could meet again." She sighed and stared out the window. After a moment, she said, "Lord Harold insists on giving us a horse. We have to accept. I can't walk very far, but I can ride."

And so it was. They left that afternoon with saddlebags full of provisions. Everyone in the manse turned out to wave them off. Garret rode along to the end of the estate, but then Malcolm and Agatha were on their own again.

Chapter Thirty

Mata Jira

The twins left Green River Manse riding two good horses.

"With the birds to help us," Malcolm said, "we should make it to Sloane's farm in a few days."

When they were on the road for the second day, they turned south.

"This is the same route I took when I left Sloane's farm riding Wee Boy, the donkey," Agatha told her brother. "We're just coming to the spot where your wolf attacked Chisel."

The road wound in curves through the lower forest.

Ahead of Agatha, Malcolm stopped his horse and dismounted. He knelt by a pile of rocks at the edge of the road. As she came up beside him, he leapt back on his horse in a sudden fever of excitement.

"Those are signal rocks," Malcolm said. "The Travelers are camped nearby! I must see if Yassif is with them!"

He turned his horse sharply onto an almost invisible trail leading off between the trees.

"Malcolm, is this wise?" Agatha called out from behind him. "Santer may still try to harm us. You already brought trouble to Yassif by attracting the panther."

"I'll be careful," Malcolm said. "We won't stay long."

But they remained with the Travelers for five days.

The Tribe's wagons were parked in a clearing higher up the mountain.

Malcolm slid off his horse and ran toward the group of people seated around the campfire. Agatha waited at the edge of the clearing.

When Yassif recognized Malcolm, he threw his arms around him, and they rocked back and forth like dancing bears. Then the others hugged Malcolm, too. There was much shouting and gesturing.

Malcolm brought Agatha forward and introduced her to Yassif and to many others whose names she didn't catch. Two women brought them bowls of warm cider, and invited them to sit on a log bench by the fire.

The Travelers wanted to hear Malcolm's adventures. While he told them his tale, Agatha studied Yassif. He was

not as large as she'd imagined. Over his missing eye he wore a kerchief that he held in place with a battered hat. His wiry gray hair was pulled back and tied into a tail.

The audience gasped with amazement when Malcolm told how Magda destroyed the panther.

When Malcolm finally ran out of story to tell, he looked around the circle of people.

"Where is Mata Jira?" he asked.

Yassif shook his head sadly.

"My mother is dying," Yassif answered. "She asked to be brought here to the mountain, to be closer to the sky." He sighed. "She will pass at the new moon."

Yassif stood up and offered his hands to Malcolm and Agatha.

"Come and greet her," Yassif said. "She knows you are here."

Inside the wagon, the old lady lay on a lower bunk. She was covered in a brightly colored patched quilt. Her cheeks were gray and sunken, but her eyes were bright.

Through Yassif, who translated her words, she spoke to Malcolm and Agatha.

"My mother says you must carry balsam for the bear," Yassif said.

"What bear?" Malcolm asked.

Mata Jira just shook her head in annoyance. She directed Yassif to a wooden chest where he removed a small burlap bag of balsam fir needles.

"These come from the trees in the far north," Yassif said. "You must keep this bag with you on your journey home."

"Curious," said Malcolm.

He took the bag, sniffed it, and handed it to Agatha. It smelled of the forest. For Agatha, the fragrance brought back memories of times long ago with her mother and father, when the family picnicked under the pines. She tucked the sack into her carry bag.

After both Malcolm and Agatha had kissed Mata Jira's hand, they returned to the campfire.

The Tribe women were now busy at a variety of tasks. Some were preparing food. A few sat weaving baskets, while others mended clothing or carved utensils from wood.

The men had moved off to a spot where they were constructing a new caravan. Malcolm and Yassif went with them.

That night, Malcolm told Agatha that the new wagon would replace Mata Jira's caravan. At her death, Mata Jira's wagon would be burned along with her body and all her possessions.

Archer and Carl stayed out of sight in the forest. Archer, of course, was supremely annoyed.

"Here you go, dallying again, while Santer digs in deeper at Hawk Hill," Archer said. "I assure you that he is not idling his time away."

Carl spent his days practicing his skill with a new game. He collected five clear stones from the nearby stream. After making a shallow hole a short distance away, he practiced tossing the stones into the hole. When he placed all five stones in the hole with no mistakes, he made a new hole further away, and started again.

In the time before the new moon, Agatha worked with the Travelers. The women busied themselves sewing quilts and weaving baskets for Yassif's new wagon. A niece of Yassif taught Agatha how to weave the baskets. Sometimes she helped the women prepare meals. Sometimes she joined the men to assist with carving and fitting parts of Yassif's new caravan.

Malcolm and Agatha stayed with the Travelers until after Mata Jira's funeral. She died as she chose, at the new moon. The Tribe fasted on that day. When darkness fell, the men pulled Mata Jira's caravan to an empty spot away from the other wagons.

Yassif built a fire underneath the caravan he'd shared with his mother. When the crescent moon appeared, he lit the wood with a torch. The wooden wagon quickly caught fire. At one point, the flames roared higher than the treetops. All watched until everything that had belonged to Mata Jira had burned to ashes.

That night, the Travelers held a feast in her honor.

The next morning, the women scraped all the ashes into a pile and buried them in a deep hole. They smoothed the earth over the spot until it was impossible to tell where the hole had been.

Malcolm was reluctant to leave. Agatha was also enjoying life with the Travelers. But Archer was pestering them to move on. And she was right, of course.

Chapter Thirty-One

The Kermodie

After the funeral, the Tribe packed up their wagons. They were heading north to spend the winter in the low country.

"Sometimes I just want to forget Hawk Hill Manse and Santer," Malcolm said, the morning that they left, "and keep traveling with the Tribe."

"Yes, I feel the same," Agatha agreed. "Or I could go back and marry Garret," she added, with a sly glance at Malcolm.

In answer, Malcolm whacked his sister with the saddlebag strap, but Agatha just laughed.

"Of course, we couldn't stay with the Travelers in any case, because of the danger that we might bring to them," Agatha said.

But the next time Santer used his magic skills, it turned out quite unexpectedly, thanks to Mata Jira.

Malcolm and Agatha parted from the Travelers when they came to the road they'd turned off days before. It was hard to say goodbye. Yassif promised he'd stop by Sloane's farm when next the Travelers passed west of the River Banneck.

Malcolm was in a sour mood. He grouched at the birds and at Agatha. She knew he was feeling low because he missed Yassif. As they drew closer to Hawk Hill, they both fell silent, thinking about how they would conquer Santer and retake their home.

Agatha sighed, and said, "I'm awfully weary. I can't imagine how we're going to fight Santer. And every day I wonder if this will be the day he attacks us again."

At dusk they made camp by a stream in the forest. Archer was barely speaking to them. She was still annoyed at the days spent with the Tribe. Malcolm caught two small trout for dinner. Carl was happy to consume the fish innards while Archer settled in a tree to eat the squirrel she'd caught.

"The fish is undercooked again, Malcolm," Agatha said. She knew she shouldn't pick on him, but she said it anyway.

"Next time *you* can catch dinner, and you can cook it, too!" he shouted, and went to wash off at the stream.

As she sat by the fire, Agatha noticed a ghostly shadow moving through the trees. She watched in frozen, terrified silence as the pale shape made a circle around the camp. Her throat went so dry that she could barely get out a word.

"Malcolm, there's something out there," she whispered. "Something white."

He hurried back to the fire. Agatha brought out her mangle. Malcolm readied his bow.

"It's a bear," Malcolm whispered. "See how it moves."

They heard it growling then, more of a muttering sort of growl than a nasty roar.

"Mata Jira told us we'd meet a bear," Malcolm said.

The bear suddenly burst forth into the camp circle. It knocked Malcolm flat with its huge paw. They had no time or distance to use weapons. With its foot, the bear pinned Malcolm to the ground while it let out a deafening roar.

The bear was too close for Agatha to throw the mangle. Even if she hadn't been too scared to move, she would have found her knife useless against such a large beast.

The white bear did not attempt to harm them further. Instead, it studied each in turn, and then continued to growl and shake its head.

"It almost sounds like speech," Agatha said.

186

"Quick," Malcolm said. "Go in my jerkin pocket and get the small carved box. Open the lid."

When Agatha opened the lid of the little box, the bear's growls turned to speech they could understand.

"I am not their servant," the bear said. It spoke in tones of anguish rather than anger. "I will not harm these young two-leggers."

"Oh, great white bear," Malcolm said, "of whom are you speaking?"

The bear lowered itself onto its haunches, removing its paw from Malcolm's chest.

"I speak of the shaman of your land," the bear answered. "He brought me here with strange magic to do harm to you. But I am the Kermodie, and I do not follow the orders of those who sow evil."

"Is this shaman named Zeddicus or Santer?" Malcolm asked.

"I do not know his name," the bear answered. "I live on the other side, in a different time and place. My home is the Great Bear Rain Forest. In my land, the shamans of the two-leggers are healers, not evil-doers."

"I thought polar bears lived in the high north," Agatha said.

The bear snorted with annoyance. "I am the rare Kermodie," it said. "I am not a polar bear. The two-leggers call me Mother Spirit Bear."

"You do look like a ghost," Malcolm said.

The bear laughed. It's a sound Agatha would never forget. She thought the Kermodie was lovely, so beautiful, and so sad.

"I am certainly not a ghost. I am as real as you," the Kermodie said. "But I do not belong in this place or time. The magic that brought me here was poorly done."

The Kermodie scanned the darkened forest. "This is not my home," she said. "These are not my trees. I cannot live here."

Two bear-sized tears fell from her eyes.

Agatha wanted to hug her or wipe her tears away with a kerchief. But she was afraid the majestic bear would be offended.

"Perhaps this will help you, Kermodie," Malcolm said. He brought the sack of balsam out of Agatha's carry bag.

The Kermodie leaned forward as Malcolm held it out to her. She inhaled deeply.

"This is the fragrance of my homeland," she said, closing her eyes. "This scent will guide me home."

The Kermodie stayed with them that night. When sleeping, she looked like a great ball of white fur with no head or legs.

In the morning, Malcolm and Agatha woke to find Archer and the Kermodie in conversation.

"I shall accompany the Kermodie as far as the land bridge," Archer told them.

"What? You're going to leave us?" Malcolm said.

"Archer!" Agatha cried. "You can't go! We depend on you!"

Archer only blinked her eyes the way she did when she had made up her mind.

"I would like to see the land of my ancestors before I return to life at Hawk Hill," Archer said.

"But this journey you're speaking of could take weeks!" Malcolm said. "Or even months!"

"The Kermodie travels with speed," Archer said. "I will rejoin you at Sloane's farm, if not sooner. The way you two have been progressing, I could be back before you've gone five miles."

She stretched out her wings, preparing to take off.

"Besides," she added, "you've got Carl. He can scout for you."

Malcolm and Agatha stared at each other in disbelief. How could they travel safely without Archer? But how could they tell her not to go?

"You expect us to depend on Carl?" Agatha said to Archer.

"Hey! Carl's done well by us," Malcolm said, defending the raven. "Remember, he found the key."

They all turned to look at the raven, who was playing his stone tossing game nearby.

"If you need a stone tossed, he's an expert," Archer said.

"Not funny, Archer," Malcolm said. "We all know Carl has limitations."

Archer stretched her wings again and stared off into the distance. It was clear that she wasn't going to give in.

"I shall return," Archer said, and lifted up into the pale morning sky.

Agatha tied the sack of balsam around the Kermodie's neck with a bit of rope.

"Safe journey, Mother Spirit Bear," she said. "I wish you could stay with us."

Then Agatha did hug her. And the bear licked her cheek in a bear kiss.

"I can travel day and night," the Kermodie said. "The gyrfalcon will return to you soon."

Kermodie

Mother Spirit Bear

Chapter Thirty-Two

The Village

After Archer and the Kermodie had left, Malcolm and Agatha were so disheartened that they sat by the cold campfire in a long silence.

Finally, Carl tired of his game. He hopped over to them.

"When do we leave?" he asked. "Has the bear gone? And where is Archer?"

"Archer is accompanying the Kermodie as far north as the land bridge," Malcolm said. "You are in charge of scouting."

Carl the Third puffed out his chest. "I shall rise to the occasion," he said. "As you know, my grandfather guarded the castle gate at the High King's court."

"Yes, Carl," Malcolm said. "We know all about your grandfather."

"He held a highly significant position," Carl said. "I shall

assume my duties and fly ahead to assure your safety."

The raven flapped away with an air of importance.

Malcolm and Agatha continued to sit for several minutes. Finally, Malcolm sighed and began to clean the campsite. He picked up the five shiny stones Carl had left near the campfire when he flew off to scout. With another sigh, Malcolm put the stones in his jerkin pocket.

They saddled and loaded the horses and resumed the journey south.

Carl did not come back.

After an hour or two, they began to look for him in the trees and by the side of the road.

"He's gone and gotten himself into a fix," Malcolm said when they stopped for a rest. "I'm sure of it."

By dusk, Carl still had not reappeared.

"We should stop now," Malcolm said. "Maybe he'll come back at daylight."

There was not much to eat. Malcolm snared a small rabbit, but without Archer's hunting assistance, they went to sleep with unsatisfied stomachs.

"I think we should be turning east soon," Agatha said as she gazed upward into the night sky.

Clouds drifted across the moon, creating a pattern of light and shadow.

Agatha had never realized how much they depended on Archer. Now that Archer was gone, Agatha felt unsafe and exposed. In addition, she had only a vague idea of the road they should take. Archer's sharp eyes could see the land in all directions from her height. She had never guided them wrong.

That night, Agatha thought a lot about Archer. She wondered why the gyrfalcon had asked to join her when Agatha first fled Hawk Hill. As a companion, Archer was opinionated and often sarcastic, but she'd always been loyal. Archer stuck by them, even when she disagreed with their choices. What, Agatha wondered, bound Archer to them? Did birds love others the way people did?

The next morning, Malcolm and Agatha were hungry and worried.

"Let's catch something to eat," Malcolm said.

"That will take all morning," his sister said. "We should move on and look for Carl."

"That blasted bird!" Malcolm said. "Whatever mess he's got himself in, let him stew in it until we've eaten."

Agatha stopped arguing. She knew they'd be less grouchy and more alert if they weren't hungry.

Malcolm went off to set a snare and Agatha wandered the stream looking for snails, crayfish, or a trout pool.

By the time they'd caught, cleaned, and cooked a rabbit and two trout, the sun was midway to noon. But they were no longer hungry or grumpy. They even agreed on the road to take eastward.

The sun was at its highest when Malcolm and Agatha came upon market day in a large village. The central commons was lined with makeshift stalls displaying all sorts of goods.

Right away, Malcolm bought four meat pies that they ate as they wandered along the booths. With one of the last of the eight gold tiffins, they bought bread, cheese, and cider to replenish the food supply.

At the far end of the commons, the two stopped to examine a blacksmith's goods. On the rickety table were several knives with ornate handles, and a brass goblet inlaid with mother-of-pearl. The merchant was a dwarf. He and three of his like were engaged in a game of horseshoe toss at the side of the booth. The dwarves were wagering with silver coins.

Next to the blacksmith's stall was a booth selling sacks of apples, pears, and baked goods. The merchant, a dwarf woman, sat on a stool beside her table. She was squat and hairy, with a broad nose and squinty eyes. And next to her, secured to the table by a rope, was Carl the Third.

Chapter Thirty-Three
The Stone Toss Game

"That's a fine raven you've got there," Malcolm said. "Where did you get it?"

"I caught him stealing my oatcakes," the dwarf woman said. "But this is no ordinary raven. This one can talk."

Agatha felt her heart sink like a stone in a pond. Not only had Carl been caught, he'd revealed that he was a rare and valuable talking beast. How would they ever rescue him?

"How much do you want for the bird?" Malcolm asked.

"Oh, this bird is a treasure," the dwarf woman said with a sly smile. "He's worth fifteen gold tiffins, at least."

By now, the four dwarves had left off their horseshoe game to listen to Malcolm and the food seller.

"I don't have fifteen gold tiffins," Malcolm said. "But I could make you a wager."

"No wager," the dwarf woman said. "I'll not sell the bird for less."

"Wait, wife," said one of the dwarves, rising from his seat on a wooden crate. He wasn't much taller standing than he'd been sitting down. "Let's hear the fellow out. What might that wager be?"

He tilted his head and studied Malcolm with a greedy eye.

Malcolm pulled five gold tiffins from his pocket. "I'll bet these five tiffins that you can't beat the bird in a game of toss."

"Beat the bird?" the dwarf said.

He exchanged looks with his companions and they all burst out laughing.

"Garg here is the best shot in the country," said his wife.

"Yes, I'm sure he is the best at horseshoes," Malcolm said. "Of course, the raven can't lift horseshoes, so you'll have to use these."

He held out his hand with the five shiny stones.

While this conversation ensued, Carl peeked sideways at the dwarves. He kept his head low, as if he'd already lost the bet. But Agatha saw that his black eyes were bright and sharp.

"And if I win?" the dwarf said.

Garg, the dwarf, may have had great aim, but he seemed to be a slow thinker.

"If you get the most stones in the hole, you keep all the gold and the bird," Malcolm said. "And if the bird tosses the most stones in, I keep the gold and the raven goes free."

"Five gold tiffins if I win, and all I lose is a pesky raven?" the dwarf Garg repeated. "Your wager is on."

Malcolm knelt down and scraped a shallow hole in a patch of flat ground in front of the stall. He made an elaborate show of measuring Carl with a piece of string provided by Garg's wife. Then he drew a line five lengths away from the hole.

"You do understand that the raven's goal must be proportionately the same as yours," Malcolm said. "Since you are five times as tall as the raven, your goal should also be five times your length's distance from the hole."

Malcolm measured Garg, cut the string, and handed it to the dwarf.

"If you like, you can measure out the five lengths yourself," Malcolm said.

Garg looked puzzled.

One of his companions spoke up. "Ya see, Garg, the raven bein' small, his throwin' distance gots to be fair for his size."

"Sure," said another dwarf, "the wager is just."

Garg took the string and measured out five lengths from the shallow hole.

"Which do you prefer, Mr. Garg?" Malcolm asked. "To toss all five in one go, or to take turns?"

Garg consulted with his fellows.

"I'll toss 'em all at once," Garg said.

"And just to show that we mean you no ill will, you may go first," Malcolm said.

By this time, word of the contest had spread through the market. A small crowd gathered around the playing area. Some folks even began to make bets on the outcome.

Malcolm handed the first stone to Garg. The crowd hushed. Garg took aim and lobbed the small stone. It landed in the hole. The bystanders cheered.

"There you go, Garg!"

The second stone also landed in the hole.

Agatha began to worry that Garg would actually win.

As Garg sighted for his third throw, a voice in the crowd called out, "Look at that fool dwarf, playing toss against a bird."

Garg's pitch went off. The stone fell short of the hole.

But the next two stones landed in the goal.

199

Malcolm started to untie Carl's leg, but the dwarf's wife objected.

"I'm not such a fool as my husband," she said. "You leave that string on the bird's leg and I'll hold the other end. I'm not taking chances on him flying away."

Malcolm gathered up the five small stones and placed them behind Carl's starting line.

"We're counting on you, Carl," he whispered.

Agatha could have been mistaken, but she thought she saw Carl wink at Malcolm.

Carl picked up the first stone in his beak. With a flick of his head, he placed the stone in the hole.

The crowd murmured in surprise.

The second stone followed the first in a perfect arc. Then the third, the fourth, and the fifth.

Garg grumbled. His companions slapped Garg on the shoulder.

"No great loss to you, friend," one said. "Only the pesky bird."

Garg couldn't help but hear the comments coming from the crowd.

"That dwarf was beaten by a bird!"

"What kind of fool takes on a wager like that?"

"He sure looks the fool now!"

Swiftly, Malcolm picked up the stones while Agatha untied Carl's leg.

"Carl, fly away now!" Agatha said, launching him into the air. "Hurry, before things get rough."

Malcolm and Agatha quickly collected the horses and rode out of the village. Soon enough, Garg would realize that he had forever destroyed his reputation as a fine sportsman. No one would forget the dwarf who lost a game of toss to a bird.

Chapter Thirty-Four

Archer

Carl was waiting for them in a tree on the eastern road. He flew down and perched on the front of Malcolm's saddle.

"What were you thinking, Carl?" Malcolm said. "Stealing oat cakes in the marketplace? We only wanted you to scout the way ahead and come right back."

Carl let his head droop. "I wanted to bring you something to eat, the way Archer does."

"That was kind of you, Carl," Agatha said. She felt sorry for him and all he'd been through. "But you won the coin toss. It turned out well, didn't it?"

Tipping his head to look at her, Carl puffed out his feathers. "Yes, I trounced that dwarf soundly!" he said. "I certainly did!"

"You would have been in deep trouble if you hadn't," Malcolm added. "You can tell us the whole story tonight. For now, do you think you can scout without getting caught?"

In answer, Carl flew off to survey their route. He came back quite soon.

"The road splits up ahead. You can either cut through the forest or go along the fens, which will take longer."

Malcolm didn't need to ask Agatha which she would choose.

"We'll take the fastest route, Carl," Malcolm said.

Soon enough, they came to the fork in the road. They could see the beginning of the forest sloping away below. In between, the road narrowed to a ribbon of rocks. The horses became skittish as they approached the rocks, but Malcolm and Agatha urged them forward. As the horses' hooves landed on the rock roadway, loud voices suddenly began to shout.

"Get off! Get off! Ouch! Ow!"

Malcolm's horse reared and twisted wildly. The sacks on his saddle came loose and went flying. Agatha's horse bucked and kicked as the voices yelled louder. Malcolm lost his seat and fell onto the stones. Agatha landed on the rocks nearby. The frightened horses galloped away in the direction from which they had come.

Beneath Agatha, the ground seemed to be heaving and rolling. The voices were deafening.

"Get off! Get off! Get off!"

"What is it?" she shouted to Malcolm over the noise.

"The rocks!" he shouted back. "We have to get off the rocks!"

Hastily, and with some difficulty, they crawled and scrabbled their way into the bushes at the side of the rocky roadbed. There they sat, bewildered and panting. Their ears rang in the sudden silence.

Cautiously, Agatha touched one of the round gray rocks at the edge of the road.

"Stop it! Go away!" it yelled.

She pushed harder at the rock. This time it lifted a bit higher and revealed the most curious face. The dome of the rock appeared to be the top of a head. Beneath was a gray face with no nose, tiny slit eyes, and a thin mouth. The eyes glared at Agatha.

"Stop poking me!" the rock creature yelled. "Leave me alone! Go away!"

It spit a pebble at her face. The missile hurt and left a red welt on Agatha's forehead. She drew back quickly.

"Yes! Go away! Go away!" other voices echoed from the roadbed.

Malcolm and Agatha did their best not to laugh.

"They may be funny, but they've spooked our horses," Malcolm said. He stood up, brushed the dust off his leggings, and stared after their mounts. "Well, do we chase them down or continue on foot?" he asked.

Agatha looked at the route in front of them, and then at the road behind.

"We might waste hours, or even days tracking the horses," she said. "It could take as much time to find them as it will take to walk to Sloane's farm."

"Or they could be grazing nearby," Malcolm said, shading his eyes and peering into the distance.

"Where's Carl?" Agatha said. "Can't he look for us?"

Malcolm and Agatha scanned the area in all directions, but could not spot the raven.

"Gone again," Malcolm sighed. "I thought he was following along with us."

He picked up the heavy sack of magic books.

"Well, at least we've still got these," he said.

"And I still have our food," Agatha added. She'd slung the carry bag over her shoulder before they set off that morning.

Careful to avoid stepping on the rocks, Agatha followed Malcolm through the bushes alongside the rock people's

road. In less than a mile, the road of rocks ended, narrowing into an overgrown dirt path.

"Not many travelers go this way," Malcolm said as they turned into the darkness of the trees.

Agatha felt a shiver of fear. So many troubles had befallen them when they passed through forests. They walked for an uneventful hour. Then Carl startled them by diving down from above.

"And where have you been, Carl the Third?" Malcolm asked.

"I was having a bite to eat," Carl said. "I found a dead deer not far off the road."

"A dead deer?" Agatha asked. Deer meat sounded like a nice change from their supply of bread and cheese.

Carl looked down at his feet. "Um—I don't think you'd want to partake. It was quite—dead."

"Oh, right," Agatha said. "Too bad."

They didn't discuss Carl's preference for carrion. It was one of the more unappealing qualities of his species.

At dusk, Malcolm made a small campfire. Agatha gathered some hazelnuts and late blackberries to go along with the bread and cheese.

They wrapped themselves in their cloaks and huddled close to the dying fire.

"I wish Archer were here," Agatha said. "I miss her."

"Carl's doing his best," Malcolm said.

"I know," she agreed. "But Archer seems to take care of so much. Even if she is a bit bossy."

Malcolm snorted. "Just a bit bossy, yes," he said, poking at the hazelnut shells. "I'm looking forward to Sloane's cooking."

"And a proper wash," Agatha added. "And a real bed."

The next morning, they woke up to find Archer perched on a low branch, preening her wings. Her feathers were darker than Agatha remembered.

"Back so soon?" Malcolm said. He was still annoyed that Archer had left them.

"Oh, Archer," Agatha said with great relief. "Thank the goddess you're here."

"Get ready," the gyrfalcon said. "Follow me."

Chapter Thirty-Five

The Fens

Flitting from branch to branch, Archer kept just ahead of them. She said nothing except to repeat her cry of, "Follow me!"

Agatha and Malcolm tramped after her through the forest for hours and hours. Carl followed along close behind, content to be relieved of his scouting responsibility.

"Shouldn't we have come out the other side by now?" Malcolm said.

"Follow me!" Archer called.

They walked until dark, then made camp. The next day, with no food left in Agatha's bag, they started out again, following Archer.

Halfway through the morning, they passed by a tree with a large, blackened gash caused by lightning.

"Didn't we pass that tree yesterday?" Agatha asked.

Malcolm only grunted, being tired from carrying the bag of books.

"Follow me!" Archer called.

Again, they set off after her.

It was late in the afternoon when Agatha tugged on Malcolm's sleeve and pointed to the same blackened tree.

"Now I'm sure that's the tree we passed before," Agatha said. "We've been walking in circles."

Malcolm and Agatha stared at Archer, who had paused in a tree ahead of them and was again calling, "Follow me!"

"What's wrong with Archer?" Agatha asked. "Do you think she's ill?"

"She does seem to have gone off her head," Malcolm said.

He called to Carl.

"Carl, fly over to Archer and have a chat," Malcolm told him. "She seems to be behaving strangely."

Carl flapped up and landed next to Archer.

They couldn't hear what he said, but what they saw was frightening.

Carl made a sudden lunge at Archer. He clamped his strong beak around her neck and shook her back and forth. Archer screamed. She spread her wings and they expanded into a huge, dark thundercloud. Then the gyrfalcon and its

gigantic black wings burst into flames. As the twins watched, horror-struck, the burning bird exploded.

Carl was blown up into the air along with hundreds of jagged blazing pieces that swirled around them like a tornado. As the sparks fell, the dry leaves on the forest floor caught fire.

"Get Carl!" Malcolm yelled, picking up the bag of books. "And run!"

Agatha squinted through the rising smoke and spotted the raven—a bundle of smoldering black feathers. Grabbing Carl, she tucked him under her arm and ran after Malcolm.

Heedless to direction, they raced through the trees. Branches whipped their faces. Brambles scratched their arms and tore at their leggings. All they could think of was outrunning the forest fire that roared and crackled behind.

At last, Agatha and Malcolm reached the end of the forest. They kept running until they had put a safe distance between themselves and the trees.

As they dashed away, they felt the ground growing spongy and wet under their feet. All around, tall reeds and grasses rustled in the wind.

"We're in the Fens," Malcolm said.

He stepped up onto a large rock, and sat down with the sack of books beside him.

Agatha climbed up next to him and laid Carl down.

"Are you all right, Carl?" Malcolm asked.

Carl raised his head briefly, and then dropped it.

"My feathers!" Carl croaked. "I can't fly. I'm no use to you now. You might as well leave me here."

"Leave you!" Malcolm exclaimed. "Certainly not!"

"Dear Carl, how can we help you?" Agatha asked.

With some effort, Carl got on his feet. He stretched out one wing, tilting his head to examine it.

"My flight feathers are badly burned," said the raven. "I won't be able to fly until after molting season." Carl stretched out the other wing. "This one is not so bad, but it doesn't matter," he said. "I shall be earthbound until after the molt."

"We'll carry you until then, Carl," Malcolm said, stroking Carl's head with careful fingers. "But if you're up to it, we'd like to hear what happened with that bird."

Carl fluffed up his poor, singed feathers. "If I could have a drink, I'll tell you willingly."

Malcolm scooped up a handful of water for Carl, who dipped his beak several times. Then the raven began.

"I flew up beside the Archer bird," he said, "and I asked her why we were so long in the forest. Are you sure of our direction? I asked her. It was the closest I'd gotten to her

since she returned from the north. I got a good look at her eyes. They weren't Archer's shiny, intelligent eyes, but the cold eyes of a snake. That's when I knew it was not Archer at all, but a magic bird conjured by Santer, or that evil Zeddicus. So I bit its neck as hard as I could, like this."

Carl clacked his beak with an angry snap to show them.

"The next thing I knew," he continued, "I was flying through the air with my feathers on fire."

"Carl," Malcolm said, "you were terrifically brave."

"You might have been killed by attacking that horrible bird, Carl," Agatha said. "And you saved us."

"The odd thing is," Malcolm said, "that the bird was leading us in circles in the forest. If Santer meant to kill us, he chose a strange way to do it."

"Perhaps Santer doesn't want you dead," Carl said. "The caterpillars, and the bunyip, and the fake Archer have only served to delay your return."

Malcolm and Agatha stared at Carl.

"It seems your recent brush with death has increased your brain power, Carl," Malcolm said. "That's a brilliant observation."

"So you mean that Santer wants to hold us off, but not kill us," Agatha said, catching on. "What could he be preparing at Hawk Hill?"

"That's the big question," Malcolm said, "and it gives me the shivers."

"I wish Archer were here," Agatha said. "She could fly to Hawk Hill Manse and spy for us."

"And I'm a useless pile of burnt feathers," Carl said, "just when you need me the most."

"Carl, you're a hero," Malcolm told him. "Far more heroic than your grandfather. All he did was guard the castle gate. You risked your life."

"What shall we do now?" Agatha asked.

Behind them, as far as they could see, spread the Fens. The grasses and reeds grew in patches between stretches of shallow swamp. It was an area most people avoided, full of snakes, frogs, and stinging plants.

In the late light of sunset, they could spot no acceptable place to shelter for the night.

"I don't want to go back into the forest," Agatha said.

"I'm done in," Malcolm said. "Let's just rest here until sunrise. Then we'll start walking east."

They covered themselves in their cloaks. With Carl nestled between them, Malcolm and Agatha gazed at the stars and dozed until morning.

Chapter Thirty-Six
Leeches

The light of the rising sun woke Agatha, while Malcolm was still asleep. She sat up and saw only tall grass. Yesterday, the edge of the forest had been visible. Today, plants taller than her head surrounded the rock. When she stood up on the rock, all she could see was grass.

Malcolm woke up and saw their predicament. Then he looked at Agatha. She was wiping away tears.

"Another delay," Malcolm said. "There's nothing to do but to follow the sun eastward."

Agatha tucked Carl into her bag, Malcolm shouldered the books, and they set off. When the sun was midway to noon, they had made no progress at all.

"This is abominable," Agatha said, wiping sweat off her forehead with the back of her hand.

They were wet and muddy up to their waists. Every part of their exposed skin was covered with red welts from mosquito bites. Agatha had seen at least twenty different kinds of large, menacing insects. A few snakes had slithered away from them. And the Fens went on and on.

"The grasses must be growing up around us," Malcolm said. "We should have been out of the Fens by now."

"Do you think this has Santer's conjuring mark on it?" Agatha asked.

"It's beginning to feel like following the fake Archer," Malcolm said.

After another miserable hour sloshing through the swamp, Agatha came to a big rock, and stepped up onto its flat, dry surface. And screamed.

"Oh, goddess! Leeches!" Both her ankles carried three or four black lumps. "Help! Malcolm! Get them off!"

Malcolm joined her on the rock. He set the bag of books down. First he examined Agatha's ankles, and then his own. "I've got more than you," he said.

"What do I do?" Agatha wailed.

"I've heard you're supposed to pull it taut near its mouth, and then slide a fingernail under it to release the bloodsucker."

"You do it!" Agatha shuddered. "I don't want to touch them."

"Oh, honestly, Agatha," Malcolm said, "are you the same woman who brought down a panther?"

"Just get them off," she said through clenched teeth.

Her good-hearted brother began to remove the leeches, one at a time.

"They aren't poisonous, you know," he said.

"I don't care," his sister groaned. "Just get them off."

When he'd gotten all the leeches off her, the punctures in her skin kept on bleeding. Agatha tore off pieces from the hem of her spare tunic and wrapped them around her ankles. Malcolm pried his leeches away, but he left his legs bare and bloody.

"There's no point in wrapping them until we get out of the swamp," he said. "We may just collect more, anyway."

The rock was warm and relatively dry, so they sat and rested for a few minutes. Agatha stared at the high reeds all around.

"Malcolm, I think I have an idea," she said. "What if we weave a wreath with the grasses, like you did to escape Zeddicus. Do you think it would end the spell?"

"We won't have hair from the warlocks' heads," Malcolm said, considering the possibility. "But if we weave

216

in our own hair, and step through, perhaps that will stop the magic."

"More fire," Agatha said. "We must be careful."

"It's worth a try," Malcolm said.

By mid-afternoon they had fashioned a large wreath of reeds tied together with long grass. Among the reeds they placed strands of their hair, and one of Carl's feathers. Jamming more reeds firmly into the mud for support, they set the circle upright.

"Are you ready?" Malcolm asked Carl and Agatha.

"I am not thrilled with the proximity of flames," Carl said. "As I think you can understand."

"I'll keep you in my bag," Agatha assured him, "and I'll hold you close."

"Hmmph!" Carl said, but he ducked deeper into the bag.

Malcolm said the spell to produce sparks. They flew from his fingers and the wreath caught fire.

Agatha jumped through first. She had expected to land in the swamp, but instead she hit solid ground—hard. When she looked back at Malcolm behind the flaming wreath, he seemed to have vanished. Agatha panicked. What if they had miscalculated, and their unstudied effort at conjuring had brought Malcolm harm? What if they were separated again?

That unbearable thought almost drove her back through the fire.

Just in time, Malcolm leaped out of the blaze.

"Ouch!" he said as he landed. "I've smashed my knees."

When the smoke cleared from Agatha's vision, she saw that they were on a narrow road. The Southern Fens were behind them, with only a plume of smoke drifting over the grasses.

She carefully pulled Carl out of the bag.

The raven stretched out his cramped wings in relief.

"Carl!" Malcolm exclaimed, "Look at your feathers!"

Carl's wings were no longer burned, frizzled stubs, but had returned to their former iridescent, fully-grown feathers.

"What good fortune!" Malcolm said. "Passing through the wreath seems to have undone the evil Archer's harm."

Carl flapped and pranced about, admiring his restored self. Then he took joyfully to the air.

"I shall scout ahead," he called, before flying away.

Malcolm and Agatha began walking eastward.

When Carl returned, he reported, "There's a farm just up the road."

Soon they came to the farm, where they bought some pears and cheese, and a bottle of ale. The farmer pointed out the road to the River Banneck.

"Sloane's farm lies on the west side of the river," he said, "just a day's walk away."

More farms dotted the landscape as they drew nearer. And then they were turning into Sloane's field.

Archer flew out to meet them, but at first Agatha didn't recognize her. She thought it was a ghost bird, possibly another one of the warlock's conjurings, and her steps slowed with caution.

The white bird with black markings landed on the pasture fence ahead of them.

"I see you lost your horses again," the bird said.

Then Agatha knew it was Archer.

"Your feathers, Archer!" she said. "You look so different!"

"These are the true colors of the arctic gyrfalcon," Archer said. "Many think gyrfalcons are the most beautiful of all the falcons."

"We want to hear about your journey with the Kermodie," Malcolm said.

"Tomorrow," Archer replied. "You look weary, and you definitely need a wash. I'll fly ahead and let the others know you're coming. My story can wait."

Chapter Thirty-Seven

Modicum Magisterium

Agatha opened her eyes, expecting to see bare branches above her head, or perhaps the pale sky of dawn. But the surface beneath her was not rocky ground, and she was strangely warm. As consciousness flowed into her, she took in the rafters of Sloane's attic, the lavender-scented sheets, and Rami's soft breathing on the pallet beside her.

At last, she was in Sloane's cozy farmhouse. Stretching her arms over her head, Agatha smiled. She was clean and comfortable, among those she loved. Whatever trials awaited with Santer, they were no longer alone.

After the morning meal, Malcolm emptied the sack of Zeddicus's books on the kitchen table.

"We must study these writings line by line," he said to Agatha. "Somewhere in these pages, we will find what we need to remove Santer."

Sloane tapped Agatha on the shoulder. "Before you begin," she said, "come with me into the garden."

When they were standing between the rows of late cabbages and parsnips, Sloane took Agatha's hand.

"It's about Rami that I want to speak," Sloane said. "The girl does strange things. She stares into the air for minutes on end, as if listening. But there's nothing there that I can see. And several times, I've come upon her talking, too."

Sloane passed her hand across her forehead.

"It's as if she's having a conversation," Sloane continued. "She speaks, then listens, then speaks again. Only she's addressing the empty air."

"How is she otherwise?" Agatha asked, with a worried frown.

"Oh, Rami's the sweetest child anyone could ask for," Sloane said. "The poor thing is so grateful to be living here and away from that beast of a father. She always wants to help, and she does her chores without being asked. And you can see how much healthier she is."

"Shall I talk to her?" Agatha asked.

"I was hoping you would," Sloane said. "Rami worships you. She is waiting for you to teach her to read and cipher."

"And I will," Agatha said. "We can begin later today. For now, I must help Malcolm search through the spell books."

221

Back in the kitchen, Malcolm sat at the table, flipping the pages of a small, leather-bound book. Rami stood beside him. Carefully, she touched a book with one finger.

"This one seems to be a history of faeries," Malcolm said. "It says here that all faeries have the power to bestow continual good fortune on those people that please them, and bad fortune on those that don't."

"I guess it's a bad idea to anger a faerie," Agatha said, pulling another book toward her.

Out of the corner of her eye, Agatha noticed Rami glancing upward, with a scowl on her face. Then the girl shook her head as if scolding someone.

"Ah, this is what Sloane was talking about," Agatha thought.

"At the end of this faerie book, it talks about negotiating with faeries," Malcolm said. "That might be useful sometime."

Agatha ran her fingers over the book in front of her.

"This one is terribly old," she said, opening the cover. "The pages are faded and ready to break apart. They're all written by hand." She peered at the first entry. "I can barely make out the words."

Rami sidled close to her, leaning forward to see.

"These seem to be recipes of some sort," Agatha said. "I can make out a list of things, like ingredients, and some numbers—maybe measurements." She turned a page. "Oh, now here's something clear. It says 'treatment for welts.' And on the next it's got 'how to manage fever.'"

Agatha looked up as Sloane entered the kitchen with a basket of vegetables.

"Sloane, you might like this book," she said. "It seems to be recipes for herbal medicines."

Sloane glanced over Agatha's shoulder at the book. "I'll take a look later," she said. "Rami, go rinse off these carrots and cabbages outside, will you please?"

Malcolm set aside the faerie book, reaching for a large, battered volume with faded gold lettering on the front.

"Now this looks promising," he said as he traced the letters. "*Modicum Magisterium.*" A moment later, he nodded. "Yes, I think this is it. The first entry is 'Spell to cause warts.'

"We'll need something a little more powerful than that," Agatha commented. "Although I might enjoy seeing Santer covered in warts."

"Shhh! Let me concentrate," Malcolm said. "Here's one to conjure snakes."

"Big poisonous snakes?" Agatha said. "That might be useful."

"Some of the components are strange," Malcolm said. "What do you suppose 'galangal root' is?"

In the afternoon, Malcolm was still poring over the *Modicum Magisterium*.

From somewhere in her storeroom, Sloane produced a slate and chalk for Rami's lessons. Agatha printed out *Rami* at the top of the slate, and watched while Rami copied her name.

When suppertime was over, Malcolm had not yet found anything useful. He rubbed his eyes and pushed the book aside.

"Oh, this tiny writing is making my eyes burn," he said.

Carl and Rami were playing toss in front of the hearth. Archer was perched on the top of Agatha's chair. Lumper pulled his chair near the fire and filled his pipe.

"Archer, let's hear your account of the journey north," Lumper said.

"Certainly," Archer said, shifting on her perch. "But please, no interruptions. And mind you, it was blessedly less eventful than Agatha's and Malcolm's journey."

Chapter Thirty-Eight

Blink

Archer began her story.

"The Kermodie moved swiftly north, and rarely stopped to rest. The bag of balsam acted like a compass, guiding her toward home. Soon the weather changed and we were making our way through snow and ice. The winter landscape was an advantage, for the bear was camouflaged against the whiteness of the snow.

"As we approached the tundra, my feathers assumed their true colors. I doubt you can appreciate the pleasure it gave me, to be rid of what felt like a disguise that I've worn for many years. An even greater pleasure was the unobstructed flight over the tundra. Impossible to describe the freedom.

"We saw few people. Only the native hunters were out on the land, fishing in the ice, or chasing down seals. The

Kermodie met up with some polar bears who shared a meal with her.

"Moving on, we reached the land bridge. The bear made her way to the middle, where a narrow strip of ice-covered land connected with a much greater chunk on the other side. She made piles of the balsam fir needles in each of the four directions. Then she began to sing and stamp her feet in a slow dance. She danced at each compass point, singing a low tune with the words, 'Hey-ya, hey-ya, hey-ya.'

"The Kermodie did this for a long time. I almost fell into a trance watching and listening to her.

"Finally, she stood up on her back legs and raised her front legs to the sky. Then she was gone—vanished in a spray of powdered snow.

"I was tempted to remain in my homeland. The freedom of it called to me sharply. But I felt my obligations pulling me southward. And so I returned."

Archer fell silent, staring with her onyx eyes into the memory of distant snows.

"Oh, Archer!" Agatha burst out. "You truly wouldn't have left us! What would we have done without you?"

"That's exactly what I mean," Archer said. "Obligations."

"But—but we love you, Archer!" Agatha said.

Archer tilted her head to look at Agatha.

"Love?" the gyrfalcon said. "Loyalty, I understand. Pride, nobility, and honor, I understand." The bird's stare was unwavering. "But love? Does the knight *love* his king? No. I am a raptor. That says it all."

Lumper leaned forward and tapped out his pipe ashes on the grate.

"Well, we're grateful that you returned, Archer," he said. "We'll be needing your help in the coming days."

Rami yawned and made her way up to the attic room and to bed. Agatha followed slowly, on quiet feet. Hearing Rami's voice, she paused before entering.

"No, Blink," Rami was saying. "You really mustn't talk to me with the others around. They'll think I'm crack-brained and send me away."

Agatha stepped forward and looked around. The room was empty but for Rami curled on her pallet.

"Who are you talking to, Rami?" she said. "Who is Blink?"

Rami stared at Agatha with huge, frightened eyes. She cowered like a rabbit cornered by a hunting dog.

Agatha knelt down, pulling Rami into her arms.

"It's all right, little one," she said. "You can tell me. No one will hurt you or send you away." She stroked Rami's fluffy, white hair. "Who is Blink?"

Rami took a shaky breath. "Blink is a tinglower."

"A what?" Agatha asked. "What's that?"

"She's a tinglower," Rami repeated. "A thing that glows."

"But I can't see her," Agatha said. "Is Blink a faerie?"

"No," Rami said with a frown. "Faeries are Little People, or the Gray Ones. They live like we do, only maybe with even more magic. They have kings and queens and everything."

"So, if Blink isn't a faerie, what is she?" Agatha asked, puzzled.

Rami pointed her finger at the rafter above their heads. "Blink is up there. She's laughing at me because I don't know the answer," Rami said, then added with a scowl, "Well, instead of laughing, you silly tinglower, why don't you help me?"

Agatha examined the rafter. She could see nothing but the wooden beam, not even a flicker of light.

Rami sighed. "Blink says to tell you that the easiest thing for you thick humans to understand is that she's a spark of spirit."

"What does she look like?" Agatha asked.

"Most of the time she's a glowing light, like a candle flame. But sometimes she likes to dress up in flowers or animals."

"And what does she do with you?" Agatha said.

"She sings songs, and tells me stories," Rami replied. "When I lived with Mam and Da, Blink stayed with me when I was sad."

"Is Blink with you all the time?" Agatha was amazed that little Rami had kept such a secret, and frustrated that she, herself, couldn't see the tinglower.

"No, she comes and goes," Rami answered. "Sometimes she has work to do. She takes messages."

"I see," Agatha said, but she didn't, really. It was hard to imagine an invisible world of light messengers carrying on around them. That was another sort of magic, different, and perhaps stronger, than conjured panthers and angry bunyips.

"Does Blink know about Santer at Hawk Hill?" Agatha asked, suddenly thinking that Rami's tinglower might be of assistance.

"Oh, yes," Rami nodded, and stopped to listen. "Blink says Santer is doing bad things to the faeries."

"What sort of bad things?" Agatha asked.

"He captured the queen," Rami said, and yawned. "May I go to sleep now?"

"Of course," Agatha said. "We can talk more in the morning."

With Rami snuggled in her arms, Agatha lay awake for a long time, wondering. Why couldn't she see Blink? What was a spark of spirit? Would they ever find a way to oust Santer?

Chapter Thirty-Nine
Crickets

"Well, I'll be!" Sloane exclaimed the next morning, after hearing about Rami's tinglowers. "Our little Grassian girl has a magic all her own!"

"It's not *my* magic," Rami said, shifting uncomfortably on Agatha's lap.

They were all gathered around the kitchen table. Lumper, Sloane, Malcolm, Rami, and Agatha, along with Carl perched on the windowsill. Archer was out on undisclosed business.

"But you have the Sight," Sloane said. "What else can you see, Rami?"

Rami shrugged. "Just Blink. And the others."

"What others?" Malcolm asked.

"The other tinglowers. Fleet and Pipple, mostly," Rami said. "But they don't come around much."

"Well, I'm relieved to know your head isn't coming unscrewed," Sloane said. She leaned over and patted Rami on the shoulder. "I was getting worried, hearing you nattering away at nothing."

"But why has Santer captured the faerie queen?" Malcolm asked. "I wonder—" he began, but was interrupted by Archer tapping at the window.

Carl flipped the catch and let Archer inside.

"I have flown over Hawk Hill," the gyrfalcon reported. "The grounds and the fields and all the outbuildings appear to be flourishing. But I could see no workers tending them. The courtyard of the manse, however, is exceedingly unkempt. I watched all morning and no one appeared but the cook and her witless son."

"And Santer or Chaucey?" Malcolm asked. "Did you see them?"

"The barn owl told me that Chaucey died some weeks past," Archer said. "No one is quite sure how he met his end. Some say it was apoplexy, while others say it was poison."

"Poor Chaucey," Sloane said. "How could he not see the evil in that Santer?"

"So I suppose Santer has declared himself Lord of Hawk Hill?" Malcolm said.

"He has," Archer said. "I dared not go close enough to eavesdrop. I would have been too easily spotted with this plumage. However, from the air I did notice a strange mist surrounding the property."

"Faerie fog," Lumper said. "I've seen it in the hills. If it's true that Santer is provoking faeries, he's taking on a fearsome enemy."

"Is Blink here?" Agatha asked Rami. "Can she tell us anything more?"

Rami pointed to the top of the cupboard. "She's up there, and she's wearing her angry parrot face." Rami waited and listened. "She says that Santer took the queen so he could make the faeries work on the farm. She says none of the people living nearby will work for him because he killed your parents."

Agatha gasped. "But how did they find out?"

"Lumper, did you or Sloane mention anything in town?" Malcolm asked their hosts.

"Not a word," Lumper said. "We haven't left the farm since Agatha set out to find you, nor spoken to anyone."

"Then it must have been Oscar, my old servant!" Malcolm exclaimed. "After he told me to escape, he probably returned to Hawk Hill."

"But don't the faeries have strong enough magic to free their queen?" Agatha asked, directing her question toward the top of the cupboard.

"Blink says no," Rami answered. "Blink says that Santer's evil is poisoning the faerie wells and ruining the faerie circles. She says it's not enough to free the queen. The faeries have been waiting for you to get rid of Santer."

"Can Blink help?" Malcolm asked. "Can she put poison in his ale?"

Rami looked horrified. "Oh, no!" she said. "That would be against the rules! Tinglowers aren't allowed to interfere with people's problems. They just carry messages and give comfort."

"Too bad," Malcolm said. "It would have made things so much easier. I guess it's back to the *Magisterium.*"

Rami was listening once more. "Blink says to tell you to look for crickets."

"Crickets?" Malcolm glanced at the floor near his feet. "Look for crickets?"

"No, silly," Rami laughed. "In the big book. She says to look for crickets in the big book."

Malcolm and Agatha spent the rest of the day side by side, reading each page of the *Magisterium.* In the evening, they continued to squint at the book by lantern light.

"Some of these spells might work," Malcolm said, "but the materials are impossible to obtain. How does one get a magus's tooth, or dragon eggshell?"

"Crickets!" Agatha shouted suddenly, startling everyone in the room. "Here it is: Spell to turn foes into crickets."

"Let me see," Malcolm said, bending close. "Willow wand, peppermint oil to conceal true motives, chive blossom to ensure victory, threads of foe's garment. Must be well-worn, not washed."

"I have all of that right here," Sloane said, "except the threads, of course."

"We should practice this spell before we cast it on Santer," Agatha said. "It must work the first time."

"Right," Malcolm agreed. "But how to get a piece of Santer's clothing? It won't be good enough to snatch a clean tunic or drawers off the clothesline. How can we get something he's wearing? Even a kerchief will do."

All the people in the room turned to look at the birds.

Archer glanced up from preening her tail feathers.

"No," she said. "I will not show myself to Santer. How about the heroic raven?"

"Yes," Malcolm agreed, "it must be Carl."

Feeling their eyes upon him, Carl turned from his spot on the windowsill where he had been toying with something shiny.

"What is it?" the raven asked. "What did I do now?"

"It's not what you've done, Carl," Malcolm said. "It's what you're going to do."

"And what are you fiddling with, Carl?" Sloane pushed up from the table to have a look. "Is that my silver thimble again?" She snatched the object away. "How many times have I told you to stop stealing my thimble?"

Carl ducked and shrugged his shoulders. "What would you have me do?" he asked. "I hope it's not fire again."

Chapter Forty

The Faerie Queen

In the morning, Sloane began to assemble the ingredients for the spell while Malcolm and Agatha coached Carl on his task.

"You must get something Santer's been wearing, Carl," Malcolm instructed. "It can't be anything clean, do you understand?"

"And you mustn't go inside," Agatha added. "It's too dangerous. Just wait until he comes outdoors."

"Yes, perhaps he'll wipe his face with a kerchief," Malcolm said. "Or leave his jerkin on a post."

"And while you're waiting, watch carefully and remember what you see," Agatha said, "so you can tell us everything."

Having repeated the instructions to the twins' satisfaction, Carl flapped away over the farmyard.

"Oh, I do hope he keeps out of trouble," Agatha said. "He's so very brave."

"Brave? That dimwit?" Archer sniffed. "Any heroics he performs are sheer coincidence. As for reporting, he can barely remember what he ate for breakfast."

"Do you have a better suggestion?" Malcolm asked.

Archer turned her sharp gaze to where Carl the Third was now only a distant, black speck in the sky.

"No," she said at last. "I suppose he'll have to do."

"Archer, while you were off communing with your ancestral lands, Carl saved us from the false falcon," Malcolm said, annoyed. "If it hadn't been for Carl, we might still be wandering in that forest."

"Hmph!" Archer said. "I think I shall see if the birds have any news of the faeries' plans." She raised her wings and lifted off into the air.

"I do believe Archer is jealous," Agatha said.

"Don't worry about Archer," Malcolm said. "We've got a spell to learn."

"How will we know we've got it right?" Agatha said. "We can't very well try turning Rami into a cricket."

"We could test the spell on Sloane's chickens," Malcolm said, gazing at the hens pecking in the farmyard.

"What would we use for threads from a garment?" Agatha said.

"Feathers, of course," Malcolm said with a grin.

Constructing the pentacle for the spell proved to be a challenge. First it was necessary to trim the five willow wands to the slimmest, unbroken strips. While Rami painted the willows with peppermint oil, Malcolm and Agatha discussed how best to tie the wands into the proper, five-pointed shape.

"If he's going to stand on it, it must be almost invisible," Malcolm said. "We can't have knots poking up all over."

They practiced making several pentacles with smaller pieces, using feathers.

"We can slip the chive blossoms into the knots at the points," Agatha said.

"And we'll use the threads from the garment to make the knots in the one for Santer," Malcolm added. "These tiny bits are awfully hard to manage. My fingers are too large."

"Let's get Rami to tie the knots," Agatha suggested.

When the pentacle was ready, Malcolm took it into the farmyard. Agatha followed, and then Rami, who stayed at a safe distance. But their first experiment with the spell was a failure. The chosen hen, placed in the middle of the pentacle, simply wandered off when Malcolm finished chanting the words of the spell.

Rami, standing by, asked, "Did you use Cackle's feathers in the pentacle?"

"Oh, no," Agatha said. "Rami's right. We have to put in the feathers of the bird we're magicking, not just anyone's feathers."

On the second try, the hen gave a squawk and disappeared, leaving a large black cricket in the middle of the star.

By the time both Malcolm and Agatha could say the spell properly, and were assured it worked, Sloane's flock of hens had been reduced to three wary birds, along with a handful of crickets.

"It's a good thing I've got a cockerel, or you all would be without eggs and roasters to eat," Sloane muttered. "I'll be glad when this business is over and done."

Carl didn't return that evening.

"Do you think he was found out?" Malcolm said as he paced the kitchen floor. "Could Santer have killed him? It would be just like Carl to get himself in a tight spot, like he did with Zeddicus's dogs and the dwarf woman from the market."

"Well, he won't be flying back at night," Sloane said, "so we might as well go to our beds." She yawned and handed a candlestick to Agatha.

At breakfast early the next morning, Carl landed outside the kitchen window. Rami opened the latch and the raven limped across the sill. He stopped, holding one foot in the air.

"What happened to your foot, Carl?" Malcolm asked.

"I had a slight brush with a rather large cat," Carl said. "But I come with news."

"Tell us," Agatha said.

Carl scanned the room, making sure he had everyone's attention.

"I shall begin when I arrived at Hawk Hill," Carl told us. "I flew to a tree in the courtyard and observed for a bit. I did what Malcolm said I should do. I picked out one person to watch and I listened hard. Only three servants were about. One is an old stableman. The others are a grouchy cook and a young man who seems to be slow in the wits. They had little to say.

"I waited quite a while, but Santer never appeared. I flew around the manse and found a broken window in one of the turrets."

"Carl! You weren't supposed to go inside!" Malcolm exclaimed.

"Well, I couldn't see anything outside. And there was a large gap in the window, so I slipped through. I was very

241

discreet. The inside of the manse is poorly kept. There's dog fur blowing about the floor, and mud on the steps. My great uncle Carlos from Iberia used to say—"

"Carl, we haven't got time for your uncle," Malcolm said. "Do go on."

"Right. Well, Santer had shut himself into a room above stairs so I took up my station on a beam in the dining hall, behind a curtain. Eventually, he came in for his evening meal. A very unpleasant fellow, I must say. Yelling at that poor boy who is obviously impaired.

"Given my task, I took special note of what Santer was wearing. He had on a leather jerkin, a loose tunic, leggings, and a fancy cap that fit tightly around his skull. He also wore a marvelous pendant round his neck, shaped like a snake coiled to strike, worked in gold. I had a cousin in India who met just such a snake, and was almost bitten. Said the serpent was deadly poisonous, but my cousin—"

"Carl, leave off about your bleedin' relatives," Sloane said. "Get on with it!"

"Yes. Sorry." Carl ducked his head. "After his meal, Santer pulled a pouch out of his sleeve. From the pouch he took some dried leaves and he threw these into the fire. The flames spread out like a curtain. Upon the flames appeared

the face of that warlock, Zeddicus. I was so startled that I nearly fell off the beam."

"Go on, Carl," Malcolm urged.

So Carl continued.

"Santer yelled at Zeddicus's face in the fire. 'The girl and her brother are at that Sloane's farm!' he screamed. 'I need your help to delay them another month!'

"Zeddicus replied that he could do nothing more. 'That wretched Malcolm stole my books,' he said. 'My old brain can't recall any more spells, neither the words nor the order.'

"'An illness then,' Santer shouted. 'At least you can send them an illness.'

"Zeddicus shook his head. 'I cannot.'

"Santer yelled so furiously that the flames wavered from the blast of his breath. 'You old fool, you've bungled everything! If I had married the girl, and your panther had done its job, the villagers would be working on the estate. As things are, no one will work for me. I can only hire incompetents for servants, and the faeries working the fields are barely under control.'

"'What's this about the faeries?' Zeddicus asked, but I have to say, he seemed weary of the conversation.

"'They're my slaves as long as I hold their queen,' Santer said.

"'Santer, you're a fool,' Zeddicus said. 'Your greed has led you to overstep your bounds.' The old warlock frowned with disapproval. "'The faerie folk have long memories for revenge,' he warned. 'And what will you do about the twins?'

"'I am waiting for them to come to me, just like a spider on its web,' Santer said. 'And they will, old man, they will.'

"The warlock's image in the flames started to shimmer like ripples on a pond. His voice wavered too, as he said, 'And do you plan to dispatch them both or keep the girl for your wife?'

"'She is no use to me now,' Santer replied. 'Once I am undisputed Lord of Hawk Hill, I shall easily procure a wife from further afield. The twins will die together.'

"Zeddicus's voice was fading along with his face. I could hardly hear his next words. 'Poison or magic?'

"'Both, old man, both,' Santer said. The fire died down, then Santer called for more ale."

Carl the Third fell silent and stretched his neck. "Do you think I might have a drink of water and a bit of food?" he asked.

"Of course, Carl," Sloane said. She brought him bread and cheese and a bowl of water.

After the raven had refreshed himself, Agatha asked, "Were you able to steal a garment of Santer's, Carl?"

"I'm getting to that part," Carl said. "When the boy brought Santer his flagon of ale, the man stretched out in front of the hearth. He took off that cap and set it on the table behind him. Then he removed the big necklace and began to study the snake, holding it up to catch the light. This was my chance. I swooped down from my perch above and snatched up the cap. He never noticed. I had my prize, but I was trapped in the hall until daylight. Santer drank more ale and studied his bauble until the fire died. Then he stumbled upstairs."

"And your leg?" Malcolm asked, "And the cat?"

Carl the Third hunched his shoulders.

"It was a miscalculation on my part," he said. "As I couldn't fly through the dark passages to find the broken turret window, I settled myself on a rafter above the hall. Who knew cats climbed that high? The feline fiend attacked me as I slept. Gnawed on my leg. I was lucky to escape with my life."

"Poor Carl!" Agatha said. "Sloane will put your foot to rights in no time."

245

"You did brilliantly, Carl!" Malcolm said. "Thanks to you, not only do we know Santer's plans for us, we also have his cap."

"You do have the cap, don't you?" Agatha said.

Carl didn't answer.

"Carl?" Malcolm said. "Where's the cap?"

"The cat took it," Carl said.

Malcolm banged his forehead on the table.

Agatha covered her face.

Carl shifted uncomfortably on the windowsill. After a long pause, he said, "There's more."

"I don't know if I can bear anymore," Sloane said. "I need a cup of tea." She opened the stove box and stirred up the coals.

Malcolm sighed. "Go on, Carl. Let's hear the rest."

"As soon as it was light enough to see, I went looking for the cat," Carl began again. "She was nowhere to be found. I suppose she had some dark corner where she made her bed. I peeked into every room or closet that wasn't locked tight. And one door opened to Santer's chamber. He was spread out on the bed, snoring. And his tunic was on the floor. So I took it."

"Do you have it still?" Agatha asked.

"Well, after a fashion," Carl said. "The tunic got a bit shredded up when I pulled it through the broken window. The sharp glass, you know."

"I'm almost afraid to ask, Carl," Malcolm said, "but where is the tunic?"

Carl flicked his head toward the window. "Out there."

"Can you bring it to us now?"

"Certainly," Carl said.

He flipped open the window latch and flew out. Within minutes, he returned with a bundle of stained, torn linen in his beak.

Agatha let out a long sigh of relief. Rami clapped her hands.

"Carl, you really are a hero," Malcolm said. "Now let Sloane put something on your leg."

"In a moment," Carl said. "I took something else as well."

The raven hopped out the window again. When he came back, he dropped Santer's necklace on the kitchen table. The coiled snake on the medallion seemed to writhe in the rays of the morning sunlight.

"Goddess preserve me," Sloane gasped, wringing her hands.

"Don't touch it!" Lumper cautioned.

The five people stared in horror at the necklace.

"We must eliminate Santer immediately," Malcolm said. "No more waiting."

"Oh, there's one more thing," Carl said.

Five pairs of eyes turned from the object on the table to stare at Carl.

"What now?" Lumper asked.

"The faerie queen," Carl said. "I saw her."

"Yes?" Malcolm said.

"In Santer's chamber," Carl continued. "There's a tall glass jar, full of swirling mist. She's in there."

Chapter Forty-One

Santer

Having decided that the spell must be cast on the following day, everyone at Sloane's farm helped with the preparations.

Sloane snipped long threads from Santer's tunic. Rami's nimble fingers tied the knots and tucked dried chive blossoms into the corners. The whisper-thin, five-pointed star of willow wand was finally ready.

Malcolm and Agatha finished packing up the spell books while repeating the cricket spell until they knew it perfectly.

From his storage room in the barn, Lumper produced a lead-lined wooden box. Gingerly, he placed Santer's necklace inside and locked the lid.

"Who knows what evil this ornament holds," Lumper said.

"We will return it to him tomorrow," Malcolm said. "Although it's a bit big for a cricket to wear."

On her pallet in the attic room, Agatha lay awake. She listened to the peaceful breathing of Rami beside her, and the comfortable creaks of Sloane's old farmhouse as it cooled in the night air.

She remembered the night she left Hawk Hill. If I'd known what lay ahead, she wondered, would I have gone anyway? And now, tomorrow, if all goes well, I will return to my starting point, at Hawk Hill. Only this time, Malcolm will be at my side.

She was still awake when Malcolm called that it was time to leave.

Malcolm and Agatha rode toward Hawk Hill Manse before dawn. They exchanged worried glances.

"So much depends on what happens now," Malcolm said.

"And think of all we've endured to get here," Agatha said, then paused for a moment. "If Santer doesn't step onto the pentacle, we can't do the spell."

"We made it as thin as we could," Malcolm replied. "It will be practically invisible in the dirt. But if the plan fails, be ready to jump on a horse and ride fast."

"It won't fail," Agatha said. "It mustn't!"

As they approached the estate lands, the rising sun illumined neatly mowed fields and carefully stacked hay.

"The faeries do a fine job," Malcolm said. "Do you think we might convince them to stay on?"

Agatha laughed.

"Have you ever seen one?" she asked. "I did once, after you left. I was sitting under an apple tree in the orchard, feeling sad. I looked up and there he was, all decked out like a courtier, in velvet and silk. He was watching me. When he caught my glance, he bowed, and then backed away into the grass."

"I never have seen a faerie," Malcolm said. "But I find I'm more curious to see a tinglower."

"Me too," Agatha agreed.

They rode on in silence.

The gate at Hawk Hill Manse was unattended. Entering the courtyard, they found a few chickens pecking in the dust.

Agatha gazed around the walls. Neglect was everywhere. The clothesline sagged from crooked poles. Someone had left a dripping bucket of slop beside the kitchen door. Bones tossed to the dogs gathered flies in the dust.

She dismounted, took a deep breath, and pounded on the oak door with the brass knocker.

Minutes passed.

Agatha pounded again.

Malcolm slid off his horse, holding the slim pentacle behind him.

Finally, a young boy opened the door a crack and peered out, bleary-eyed.

"Wha' is it?" he said. His tunic was filthy, as was his face. He wiped his nose with the back of his hand.

"Fetch your master, please," Agatha said. "Tell him Agatha wishes to speak to him."

The boy blinked and gaped.

Agatha repeated herself.

He still stood there, gawping.

"Go. Get. Your. Master. Now." She stepped closer.

He went, shutting the heavy door.

Malcolm set the pentacle in front of Agatha, making sure to blend it into the dirt. Then he mounted his horse, holding Agatha's mangle on his saddle in readiness.

From behind the door they heard echoing shouts and heavy footsteps.

Santer flung the door open. He had dressed in haste. His hair was rumpled but his eyes were knife-sharp.

"So you've come at last," he said. "I knew you couldn't stay away."

Agatha took two steps back. Even though she had expected to see him, she still felt a shiver of fear in his presence.

"We've come to claim our land," she said.

"Come inside," Santer said, gesturing to invite them in. "We have much to discuss."

He turned and called out, "Boy, have the cook bring some bread and ale to the hall."

Agatha cast a worried glance at Malcolm. They had to get Santer to step out of the door. The only sound for several seconds was the clucking of the chickens.

From astride his horse, Malcolm said, "We have a bargain to propose, Santer."

"A bargain, is it?" Santer grinned, showing his yellowed teeth. "And what might that bargain be?"

"You give up Hawk Hill Manse for the books I have in this sack," Malcolm said, patting the bag tied to his saddle.

"Hawk Hill Manse for a bag of books? That sounds like a lopsided trade," Santer sneered.

"Then perhaps this might sweeten the deal," Malcolm said. He brought out the lead-lined box, opened the catch, and held up Santer's necklace.

"How did you get that?" Santer growled. He narrowed his eyes with suspicion.

253

"Never mind how," Malcolm said. "Perhaps we have more power than you think," he added, returning the necklace to its box. "But see what I have with me here."

Malcolm removed one of Zeddicus's spell books from the bag. He knew he had to get the distance exactly right or the cricket spell wouldn't work. Urging his horse to step forward, Malcolm leaned toward Santer, offering the book just a few paces away.

Santer's eyes gleamed. He flicked his tongue over his lips.

"You little thief," he said. "You stole the *Modicum Magisterium.*"

He licked his lips again, stepped forward, and snatched the book from Malcolm's hand.

Agatha stifled a gasp.

Santer was standing inside the pentacle.

Chapter Forty-Two

Hawk Hill

Santer opened the leather-bound book with greedy reverence while Malcolm and Agatha muttered the words to the spell.

The warlock looked up from flipping the pages in time to see Agatha's hands making the sign that sealed the magic. His shout of rage echoed off the walls of the courtyard. Dropping the *Magisterium* in the dust, Santer whirled in a circle, expecting an attack. When none came, he lunged at Agatha. She leapt backward.

Santer raised his arms, as if to conjure a spell. "You will die now!" he shrieked. Then he stiffened.

"AAK!" Santer screamed.

The warlock's scream became a shrill whistle. He froze, staring at his arms that were turning into black insect legs. His face registered shocked disbelief. Black antennae

sprouted from his forehead. His eyes turned black and divided into multiple lenses. He shriveled and shrank. Soon, nothing was left of the man but a pile of clothes.

Malcolm and Agatha stared at each other in the silence of the early morning.

"That was truly horrible," Agatha said, letting out the breath she'd been holding. She poked the empty garments with her toe.

Out hopped a large, black cricket. Before Agatha could step on the insect, a hen dashed forward, scooped up the cricket in her beak, and swallowed it.

"So our parents are avenged," Malcolm said.

"And the evil murderer comes to an ignominious end," Agatha added.

Malcolm slid off his horse and stood beside her. She took his hand and they turned to gaze at the manse.

Before them, the kitchen door glided open, emitting a lilac mist. Stepping out of the mist came the faerie queen. She was slim and tall, with swirling black curls and a gown of purple water beads.

From the fields behind the twins came strange, high sounds, like a roosting flock of starlings. Soon, dozens of faeries were pouring in through the gate, singing and cheering.

In his hands, Malcolm still held the lead-lined box with Santer's necklace inside.

He stepped forward and knelt at the feet of the faerie queen.

"Your Highness," Malcolm said, "I beg you to take this with you. We know not what evil magic powers it contains, but I think you and your people are best equipped to manage it."

The faerie queen bowed, accepting the box in her hands. She then turned and handed it to a courtier. He looked very much like the faerie gentleman that Agatha saw three years ago.

"Thank you for your courage, young lord and lady," the faerie queen said. "You have lifted the evil man's poison from our lands. For this act, your crops will always be plentiful, and your fortunes good."

The faeries gathered around their queen, shouting and dancing, and throwing hats into the air. They escorted her out of the courtyard. Then, as suddenly as they appeared, they were gone.

Malcolm and Agatha were once again alone in the quiet courtyard.

A rush of wings announced the arrival of the birds. Carl landed on Malcolm's saddle. The gyrfalcon perched on the carved lintel above the oak door.

"Well, don't just stand there," Archer said. "Get to work! This place is a frightful mess."

About the Author

Kim Ellis began her writing career with a red crayon under her parents' coffee table. At age four, she upgraded to the closet door. Now, as a retired teacher, she is still scribbling away, producing stories that have appeared in *Cricket, High Five Magazine for Children, Stinkwaves,* and *Skipping Stones* magazines. She won first prize for children's poetry in *Children's Writer Newsletter* (February 2014). Kim is a teacher consultant with the Hudson Valley Writing Project. She enjoys yoga, quilting, and hanging out with her granddaughters. *Tangled in Magic* is her first published book.

Thank you for purchasing and reading *Tangled in Magic*, Book One of *The Karakesh Chronicles*.

Handersen Publishing is an independent publishing house that specializes in creating quality young adult, middle grade, and picture books.

We hope you enjoyed this book and will consider leaving a review on Goodreads or Amazon. A small review can make a big difference for the little guys.

Thank you.

More books from
Handersen Publishing, LLC

Also from Handersen Publishing

Cover Art By
Raven Howell

Interview With
Author, Alex Henson

Featured Authors
Alex Henson
Rebecca Linam
Scott Merrow
Theodora Morley
Jeffrey G. Roberts
Elizabeth J.M. Walker
Sephone Zorro

Featured Artists
Rhea Baxter
Allen Forrest
Jane Gregoritch
Jessica Hillegeist
Raven Howell
Denny E. Marshall
Cesar Valtierra
Matthew Wall
Shannon Wall

Featured Poets
Jaha Batainch
Raven Howell
Ginny Kaczmarek
Herb Kauderer
Denny E. Marshall
Peter MacQuarrie
Philippa Rae
Lily Tierney
Damian Wakefield

Stinkwaves
Magazine
Spring 2017
Volume 5 Issue 1

Stinkwaves started in 2013 as a zine, but has now grown into a "mega-zine" filled with the works of talented indie authors, poets & illustrators. Each issue is packed with short stories, flash fiction, poetry, illustrations, and author interviews.
www.stinkwavesmagazine.com

Handersen Publishing

Great books for young readers

www.handersenpublishing.com

Made in the USA
Columbia, SC
14 November 2017